ANIMAL

# Animal

STORIES BY

*Alexandra Leggat*

ANVIL PRESS • VANCOUVER

Anvil Press Publishers Inc.
P.O. Box 3008, Main Post Office
Vancouver, B.C. V6B 3X5 CANADA
www.anvilpress.com

LIBRARY AND ARCHIVES CANADA CATALOGUING IN PUBLICATION

Leggat, Alexandra
    Animal : stories / Alexandra Leggat.

ISBN 978-1-897535-01-1

    I. Title.

PS8573.E461716 A75 2009     C813'.54     C2009-900257-4


Printed and bound in Canada
Cover design by Mutasis Creative
Interior design by HeimatHouse

Represented in Canada by the Literary Press Group
Distributed by the University of Toronto Press

The publisher gratefully acknowledges the financial assistance of the Canada Council for the Arts, the Book Publishing Industry Development Program (BPIDP), and the Province of British Columbia through the B.C. Arts Council and the Book Publishing Tax Credit.

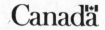

"For Tate"

# Table of Contents

Wide » 9

Apples and Rum » 15

Animal » 39

The Last Monsoon » 43

Scimitar » 55

Kid Airplane » 67

Fuselage » 75

Tourniquet » 85

Mandible » 95

Over Dinner » 105

Sweet Tea » 107

The Market » 119

Blue Parrot » 127

Colt 45 » 155

# Wide

IN THE BACK ROOM, Jess arranges nails by length. Counts and recounts metal after metal prong, keeps an inventory. Never uses them.

"Save the long ones for my coffin," I say.

His pale brown eyes scream at me. They're the only voice he has left.

I slam the jars I'm holding onto the counter. The cucumbers I've been pickling turned purple. I'm tired of the inadequacy of the recommended organic products, the ambiguity of natural ingredients.

Jess appears at the pantry door, fists clenched, cheeks red. He stomps his left foot. I raise my eyebrows. He charges out the door to the middle of the yard, drops to his knees and pounds the ground. He's pounding too hard. I run to his side and grab his arms. He bruises easily. His hands turn blue from the blows. He closes his eyes.

"Let's walk," I say.

I yank him to his feet and we trudge through the cornfields

to the side of the unpaved road horses pull carriages on. We spot a man with a beard, blue trousers, shirt, and black, wide-brimmed hat. He's standing in a field across the road, gazing at the sky. Jess points to him. I tell him it's not polite to point. He glares at me. I apologize. We communicate the only way we know how.

The man turns his head and notices us. Jess takes a step back. The man smiles, walks to the edge of the road and we look at each other. He glances around then waves at us. I wave back. Jess stands behind me, grips my hips with his bruised hands. The man grabs his hat and runs into the field, keeps running until we can't see him anymore. Jess teeters on the side of the road, strains his eyes. He looks up at me.

"He had to go," I say.

Jess takes off toward home. I can hear his hands slapping the corn as he rushes past it. I plod after him.

In the back room the nails are scattered across the floor. Jess's logbook of numbers is torn and scrunched into a ball. He appears in the doorway. Claps his hands. I gather the mess and place the nails in a red tool box I bought for other things. He doesn't protest the mixing of the nails. He's already forgotten that he laboured over separating them.

I dig through the cupboards, find crayons and an old sketch book that I used to write recipes in. I could never draw. I hand them to Jess. He drops to his knees on the kitchen floor. I wash the dishes. The sun sets over the pond I had drained to save his life. My stomach grumbles. I want to eat out, steak, baked potato, sour cream.

The school bus stops at the end of our driveway. The red lights bounce off the windows. Jess bats his eyes to the rhythm. He loves the colour red. I told him if he behaves himself, I'll get him a fire truck, a real one. I look back at the pond, the sky. The sun's setting too soon. School kids lumber down the road and into their homes.

"Jess, I want to move to the city."

He pounds his fist on the linoleum. I shove my foot under it. He lurches to his feet and opens his mouth like a lion. It's perfectly round, a toothy full moon. Wide but silent. I lead him to the couch, turn on the TV. Through the window I watch a man get out of a small silver car and cut branches from a fir tree. His lips are moving. Jess's eyes close. I turn up the volume on the TV, the buzz puts him to sleep. His head drops to his chest. He sputters as he snores.

The evening air is cool. I button my cardigan, shove my hands into my pant pockets, tuck my hair behind my ears. The man's suit is neatly pressed, car gleaming. His hair is a little longer in the back, around the ears, wavy. It looks like chocolate.

"Are they for a girl?" I ask.

He jumps and turns around, drops the trimmings onto the gravel shoulder of our newly paved road.

"You scared me."

"I'm scary?"

"No. I don't know."

I kneel down and pick up the branches. I can see my reflection in his shoes. My eyes are sparkling and my lips are fuller than I thought. He's tall. I reach up to him and hand him his cuttings. It's not my tree so I don't care what he's done. It's the earth's tree. Let's see how it handles him. There's a suitcase on the backseat of the car.

"If you add red branches to the fir, it looks pretty. I can get you some, come out back with me."

"This is good."

"Just give me a minute, I'll get you some."

When I run up the driveway, I hear his car pull away. There's no point in watching him go. Jess is not on the couch. The TV's turned upside down. A stream of smoke drifts out its back. I unplug it and put my back to the wall. I listen for footsteps, heavy breathing. In the mirror I notice the screen door swinging in the wind. I race outside. Clouds gather above my head, conspiring, telling secrets, spreading rumours.

"It's not true," I scream.

There's no sign of Jess. Nothing. No moans or sobs loping out of the tree house he built twenty years ago for a son that never happened. He was so industrious then, but he's not hiding in his handiwork. I run through the corn fields. I don't like it when things tower over me. Jess is small and I prefer small men. I can't tell if it's my breath or the corn's heaving in my ears.

The husks are proud of themselves. I'm not oblivious to their remarks. I hear their whispers but can't make out what they're saying. When I find him, that's it. The corn and the clouds are eyeing me in the way women eye each other.

"Jess?"

I hear snorting, the clip clop of hooves against asphalt.

"Jess?

The wide-brimmed hat that had sat on the nice man's head lay upon the road. He is nowhere in sight. The tail end of a horse disappears over the hill. In my bare feet I run across the road after it. My gut's screaming, telling me there's a problem, a big problem, and that the horse and the hatless man are not happy. When I reach the top of the hill there is nothing but dust in front of me. That man should never have waved to me across the road—he should have kept his eyes averted. Jess does not react well to another man's presence. I think of the guy in the silver car, and the overturned television. The sun stretches across the opaque sky. In the clouds, I can see the backs of angels.

# Apples and Rum

BEN REMOVED MEG'S boxes from the trunk; precious glass and china ornaments, wedding gifts, heirlooms, books and art not to be trusted with moving companies. Ben had discarded most of his belongings at a garage sale, which Meg found odd for a man who hung onto receipts from his previous marriages. She strolled into the living room, removed her shoes and walked barefoot on the hardwood floors. Windows covered three of the four walls. A wood burning stove sat in the corner, its front like a gaping mouth. A wrought iron spiral staircase led downstairs to the den, and a second bathroom. She climbed back up the stairs, running her hand along the cool banister, heart pounding. She pictured the entire house decorated, full of friends, laughter. In the master bedroom she threw her arms above her. This is all mine, she whispered, and gazed through the window that led to nowhere or everywhere for all she knew. A red-tailed hawk drifted across the field in front of her, its talons outstretched, body hunched, wings lowered. Meg awaited the kill. The hawk dove into the long grass and disappeared. Until that moment everything around her was alive. Any doubts she had about the move, change, risk, shot out the bedroom window into the field to be ravaged with the voles.

She'd yearned for change, a home away from everything, a chance to breathe fresh air, to scream at the top of her lungs if she wanted to without neighbours hearing and gossiping about it with other neighbours, who stared at her through bay windows when she took out the garbage or wept on the doorstep. When she felt the walls closing in, hers and everyone else's, she'd drive to the country for refuge. She desired an old yet updated home with enough space to stretch out but not lose Ben in. The house found her. It was there at the foot of a sloping hill, waiting to be bought. After much nagging and weeping and slamming of doors, Ben relented to the move.

She joined Ben by the car. He was humming. He never hummed. It wasn't his nature. The hawk emerged from the long grass and soared over them.

"You never know what's looming above you, Ben. Life can change in an instant."

She chuckled. He stopped humming. She made him self-conscious. With the onset of a drooping profile and extended belly, he'd made numerous comments about his shrinking confidence. A smirk eased across his solemn face. She knew he loved her but sensed he was at a crossroads, uncertain of anything. At their farewell party, she overheard him mention something to a colleague about the attainment of reason. He whispered to the fellow that he needed to find himself a comfortable existence to live out his remaining years. With this she thought the move, the house, was perfect. She too was changing. Couldn't take the traffic, all the traffic, human and metallic, noise, smog, and the overwhelming sense of emptiness holding court. She'd exhausted the social scene, and once the city had begun to bore her, she yearned to be amidst the natural world. That Ben would relent and embark on rural life astounded Meg, but she refused to lose sleep questioning situations where she came out on top.

Side by side, they stared at the stone house they'd purchased for half the price of something newer nearer the city. The dog pranced around, ears pricked, nose moving like a rabbit's. Ben leaned against the car, wiped the sweat from his forehead and puffy cheeks. He lit a cigarette. Meg ventured into the vacant red barn. Inhaled the remnant scent of horses. She loved barns, something about their shape, their general aesthetic, the way they loomed with purpose upon an outstretched field. A hum drifted through the open wooden doors, a welcome breath of wind whistled in. Probably passes through every day at the same time, thought Meg. She'd look forward to its daily caress.

She wandered into the kitchen, removed the cleaning products from a canvas bag, products she bought but rarely ever used. She scrubbed the counters, the fridge, and spread patterned shelf liner upon the cupboard shelves. Through this she hummed.

Ben sat on the front porch smoking, indifferent to his new surroundings, checking his Blackberry. Smoke drifted in through the kitchen window. Meg hated it when he smoked. She worried about his health. The last thing she wanted was to have an illness ruin the good of their new lifestyle. She hoped retirement would curb his cravings, but it seemed to make him more anxious. His eyes were peeled to his phone and Meg suspected he was considering one of a flood of consultancy offers he'd received when news spread he was leaving his teaching position. In the back of her mind, Meg knew he'd die working—some people can't stop. He told her that when everything else winds down, work is what reminds him he's still alive. Meg believed that he tried too hard. If he could just let go, take up gardening or even write a goddamn book, anything to keep him home.

The dog howled. Meg headed out onto the front porch. They were expecting the moving van and were surprised to see a rusty old tractor making its way up the driveway. Puffs of smoke billowed behind it. A tall fair-haired man in overalls leapt off the tractor and approached Ben with a smile, extending his right hand.

"I'm Samson," he said.

Then he jogged back to the rusting machine and grabbed a bushel of newly picked apples and a forty of dark rum. His smile glimmered through his gifts. Meg took in his sturdy build. Ben introduced his wife. Samson nodded, eyes averted, mouth taut. She invited him in.

"I live a few acres over, in the white house," he said. "Been in that house since a kid, apple farmers mostly around here but things are changing. I'm so happy to see a new couple occupy the place."

Ben unpacked tumblers and removed an unopened bottle of Coke from the still-warm fridge. "It'll spray," Meg said, and it did, all over the newly cleaned counters and floors. Samson and Ben had a good laugh. Meg took a deep breath, wiped up the mess. What did it matter, she thought, the old house had new friends in it, why make a fuss?

"Cuba Libres for all," she said and plunked a slice of lime in each glass. Samson leapt to his feet, shook his finger at the drink. He was horrified. He only ever drank dark rum on the rocks with a slice of his juicy apples. He told them that his father drank the same concoction in the heat with the Jamaican farmers he'd recruited from a one-off vacation. The orchards thrived then, attended by hard-working hands that weren't afraid to ache.

Samson's father had to let go of the hired help when even cheap labour became too expensive and farmers relied more and more on their offspring. But the young had changed. Getting their hands dirty, rising early, or following in a father's footsteps held little to no appeal. An only child, Samson relented. He sipped his drink, shook his head. Meg and Ben exchanged glances. Samson explained his predicament: no money to keep up his farm but he couldn't bear letting it go to be torn apart and made into vineyards. It's a bleak sight, he said, when the hauled-out roots of old apple trees are bared to the merciless sky then set ablaze in huge piles by the side of the road.

Meg hung on every one of Samson's words, watched his eyes grow moist. Ben removed his glasses and took a different interest in what was being said. She opened her mouth but instead it was Ben's words that bellowed across the kitchen she'd looked forward to having good conversations in. She backed away and entered the living room where she sat in the bay window drinking a beer she'd snatched from the cooler. Her husband and the apple farmer conversed like they'd known each other for years. Ben thrived in the company of men. She heard more rum gurgling into their glasses. Smelled the apples as Ben sliced them without a cutting board on her precious new counters. The sun gradually lowered upon the old tractor. Not one to be alone during a good sunset, Meg returned to the kitchen.

"It must be so hard to devote your life to a career that depends on the weather," she said. Samson nodded. She reached for another a beer. Ben waved her out of the room. She was beginning to despise apples and rum. The men finished the bottle. Samson stood up, red-faced and grinning, shook Ben's hand then threw his arms around him like the long lost brother he never had and said he needed to fill a few more bushels before nightfall. Meg shook his large chafed hand and asked if he needed help. She'd never been apple picking. Only ever chose them from a polished pile in an overpriced grocery store. Samson smiled at her like he must have smiled at his mother. He left his phone number, told Ben to call if they needed anything and roared across the fields. A puff of smoke rose above him.

"He's so alone," said Meg.

"On the contrary," said Ben.

Once the furniture arrived and Meg had spent time organizing the house, she dragged Ben to an auction in town where they purchased two secondhand racehorses with no papers, a used tractor, six hens, a cock, and a goat. She'd always wanted horses and the goat won her over when it stood on its hind legs and leaned on the fence, luring her in like an old movie actor. On the way home Ben asked to be dropped off at Samson's. She wondered why but didn't ask. She didn't want to annoy him after the gifts he'd bought. It had been too good a day to end it alone. When they pulled up by the tractor, Samson bounded from his barn. He grabbed Ben's hand and shook it. They walked toward the house laughing. Meg wondered if this was how a mother felt when she dropped off her kid. The second they leave the car, the mother's forgotten. They don't even turn around to wave goodbye.

Meg drove home to await the arrival of the animals. She'd cleaned the stalls, loaded up on bedding, hay and oats. Old tack was bought from a farmer who'd lost his horses to a fire. It saddened Meg to use their tack but figured it was a way to let the forsaken creatures live on.

Sweating and snorting, the horses arrived. Meg helped the

handsome young man in Levis and a black tank top remove them from the trailer. They led the glistening creatures into their respective stalls and the young man told Meg to call if she needed anything. She was thrilled when she twigged to looking younger than she felt. He moved closer to her and handed over his card. She studied his steady eyes and whispered, "You better be careful what you wish for, kid."

He took a step back, stared at her, then got into his pickup and drove away. She hooked onto his eyes in the sideview mirror, winked at him. She was hedging her bets and she knew it, something about the wide open spaces and a husband that had barely been around since they arrived. It amazed her that no matter where they were—in a grocery store, on vacation, home—he always managed to escape.

She strode into the house. Her footsteps echoed. Light filled the bright white kitchen. The cupboards touched the ceiling and stretched down to the counters. It was a daunting sight, but she knew that cooking was only a matter of time, something she was ready to take on. The kitchen both petrified and enticed her, like men she'd adored but never attained, and she wondered if anything ever changes. She opened the full fridge looking for a drink. Bundles of fresh food that she hadn't had a chance to prepare stared back at her. She called Samson and invited him and her husband for dinner. Samson explained that they were knee-deep in charts and bank statements and a meal would be a welcome break.

She lit candles, polished cutlery, set the brand new kitchen table they'd purchased in town. A bottle of half-drunk Merlot rested on the counter and the aroma of the almost-cooked beef filled the house like the country feast of a big and happy family. She sat on the couch and sipped her wine, listened to the clock tick. The dog cleaned his paws by the crackling fire.

Samson arrived out of breath, a speck of blood on his cleanly shaven face and his sweet-smelling hair slicked back.

"Ben's on his way," he said.

"What's he doing?"

"He's so much better at numbers than I am."

"He likes to keep busy."

"He's saving me."

She stopped breathing, until she realized that she had stopped breathing. A slow heat crept into her temples. Samson tiptoed around the dog. He was tall, handsome. His biceps exited the sleeves of his black T-shirt like she wished Ben's would.

"A glass of wine?" she said.

"I brought rum."

She took the bottle and went into the kitchen. He followed her with an apple. She sliced it and plunked it into his tumbler.

"He saved me once, too, you know. He's good at it."

Samson nodded. He strolled into the living room, looked up and down the bookshelves, the artwork, the furniture. He ran his hand across the distressed leather couch, read the spines of books hoping to recognize something, inhaled Meg's perfume through the equally alluring aromas of beef and firewood. He glanced over at her, studied her small frame and smooth face, wondered what Ben had saved her from. An even older man? Meg screwed the top onto the rum, felt the fire in her veins burn out. The front door flung open. Ben entered the house wide-eyed and grinning.

"Well," he said, "what's going on? Are you having a good time?"

Samson turned and stared at him. Meg placed Samson's drink into his stiff hand.

"We were waiting for you, honey. Why have a good time without you?"

At the table, Ben did all the talking. Talked like a mad man, exuberance spewing from his full mouth. He inhaled beef, fennel, sweet potatoes, carrots, onions, bread, wine, and rum. Spent the entire dinner urging Samson to relent, to purge the apple trees, revamp the orchards altogether. Think of the money, he said, the freedom. Meg guzzled her wine and barely looked up. When she did, she noticed Samson sat there immobilized. Through the folds of his eyes she spotted a tenderness that rankled her nerves.

"What do you say we go for an after-dinner drink?"

Samson shook his head. She offered to drive them to one of the local bars.

"A night on the big town, boys, what do you say? Samson, come on, let's go out, the three of us. Forget about the farm for a night."

"Being in public makes it worse," he said. "The locals are vultures."

"It's not about the people, Samson, we're going for the booze. We'll drink in the corner."

Ben stopped chewing, thumped his hand on the table. "That's a great idea. Come on, Samson, take my young wife out for a drink."

Meg almost choked on her wine. Samson downed his rum, thanked Meg for dinner and hurried to the door. Meg got up to say goodnight but he rushed through the door without turning around.

"What the hell was that, Ben?" But Ben was no longer seated at the table. She blew out the candles.

Ben had moved into the living room, removed his spectacles from his head and placed them on his rose-tinted nose. His head was buried in a large hardcover book.

"You spend too much time with your head in books," said Meg.

He flipped the pages. At his feet were piles of papers, studies on the marginalization of crop farmers—stats, essays. Meg stooped to pick one up and Ben placed the heel of his shoe on it. Blue and green lines stood out, shapes of places, large bodies of water, mountain ranges.

"What's this?" she asked, sliding the map out from under Ben's foot.

He grabbed it from her.

"It looks like a map of France," she said.

"So it does. I'm studying the wine regions."

She kneeled down, stared up at her husband. He had never been young in her eyes.

"What are you doing, Ben?"

"Samson is wise in the ways of the earth, Meg, but of business he knows little. I've weighed the pros and cons of defying the changing trends and the numbers don't fall in his favour. Think of the wine you'll have."

"Me?"

"Samson, you, the community."

"He has no affinity with grapes."

"Honey, I have everyone's best interests at heart. Trust me."

"Trust you?"

Her throat tightened. Since moving into the house of her dreams, he was never home, crawled into bed when she slept, and was gone when she awoke. With Samson he talked non-stop over rum and his ridiculous apples and cigarette after cigarette after cigarette. He stomped to and from Samson's, incessantly checking his Blackberry. What was he waiting for, a bulletin from heaven, something to beam him up and out of there? She sought solace in the dog, the horses. She'd saddle one up and gallop into the fields weeping. Ears flat against its head, the horse she rode ran harder and harder in an attempt to escape the hysterical woman on its back. She went to bed and stared at the ceiling until she heard Ben coming up the stairs and into the room.

"Do you wish we hadn't moved, Ben?"

She startled him.

"No, it's good. You're happy, aren't you? Isn't this what you've always wanted? I want to give you everything you've ever wanted."

Her gut wavered. What the hell was he talking about?

"And look at the wonderful neighbour you have," he continued. "He's such a nice young man, Meg. Trust me, he'll be very wealthy when I'm finished with him. How about that? A handsome, reliable man, right next door."

"Ben . . ."

He placed his glasses back onto his nose and went downstairs. She counted backwards from one hundred until she fell asleep. Something she'd done since she was a child. When she awoke, Ben was sleeping beside her with his mouth open. She slipped down to the kitchen, hushed the dog. She put the coffee on, reached into the fridge for fruit, bacon, eggs. She hummed, scurried across the cool tile floor. The sun peeked through the side window.

"What are you doing?" asked Ben.

Meg jumped, dropped an egg. The dog howled, fulfilling its morning ritual. Fully dressed, including his loafers, Ben stood in the doorway with a pile of papers shoved under his arm.

"Making breakfast. Spend the day with me, Ben. We'll ride out to the river, I'll show you where the coyotes live. I found a den. I know they're there, somewhere. Spend some time with me, Ben. Please, that's all I want."

"I have to help Samson," was all he said, and left on foot, shoulders raised to his ears and a cigarette dangling from his crinkled mouth. Meg whipped an egg at the door. It limped down the white paint. She ran to the barn, saddled up Tex and rode to the river. She leapt off the horse. Snorting, sweat foaming on its sinewy neck, it trotted a few feet away, ravaged the long grass while keeping a frantic eye on her.

Throwing sticks into thick water, she retraced the steps that removed them from the city. She thought it was because of the overpopulation, the smog, their incestuous circle of friends, the cost of living, car alarms. She'd tired of socializing with Ben's scholarly associates—number-crunchers, economists, bankers, accountants. They rarely included her in their conversation. She was convinced that after the shock of Ben marrying for the third time to a much younger woman, they ceased to acknowledge her existence. She wanted free of their scrutiny, to stand by her husband on equal footing. She thought he'd wanted that too. She pulled at her hair, attempted to piece together the signs, the symptoms. She was never good at numbers. She stared at the murky river. It gave her nothing, not even a reflection to contemplate.

They returned to the barn. She unsaddled Tex and led him into the swaying field. Coco trotted to his side. He looked relieved to be home. She grabbed a beer from the little fridge

Samson had installed for her in the tack room, sat on the fence and gazed through the bare trees, wondering what it was that intrigued her husband so much about saving the apple farmer in need.

The sky was changing, closing in. She shivered and made her way inside. She made a stew and shared it with the dog. The silence became too heavy. She grabbed the car keys, drove to Samson's and spied through his window. Ben and Samson were sitting at the kitchen table talking. She couldn't bring herself to knock on the door. They stood up and shook hands. Meg ran to the car and drove back home with the lights off, relying on the moonlight to guide her.

Perhaps Ben was buying Samson out, she thought. It's a surprise. His new project. He'll relieve the poor guy of his burden once and for all. She fell asleep without counting backwards. Meg awoke from a warm dream. A guy she used to know wanted her so badly that he acted on it. It was cool and dark, smelled of rain. She opened her eyes to find Ben packing a suitcase at the end of the bed. He must have assumed she'd sleep through it, the thumping on the bed. A movement she was no longer accustomed to, but couldn't imagine not being roused by.

"Honey," she said, "are you going somewhere?"

He shushed her. Placed one of his long knobby fingers over his cracked lips. Without looking up from his folding he said, "I've thought a lot about this, Meg. I've accepted a teaching position at the Sorbonne. The offer came up before we left but I didn't want to ruin the good of your new life."

"The Sorbonne. The Sorbonne? The Sorbonne is in France."

"Yes, Meg. I'm going alone."

She sat up, rubbed her eyes, checked her wrists for a pulse; it was there. Checked her heart for a beat, a bullet hole.

"You're retired, Ben. You don't teach anymore."

He didn't move, just stared at the neatly packed suitcase.

"You don't speak French! Jesus Christ, Ben. What the hell is going on?"

He shook his head. Samson relied on Ben's companionship and in Meg's plea to stop him from leaving she tried to explain that she wasn't the only one he'd be letting down.

"Honey," he said, "aren't you happy? You have everything that you've ever wanted. A house in the country, horses . . ."

"You keep mentioning that."

"Freedom."

"Freedom? I didn't mean that kind of freedom, Ben. Freedom from the establishment, sure."

He placed his hand on her chin. "You're a young woman, Meg. I was a fool to think I could be anything more to you than a patron."

"What?"

"This is all yours, dear. A gift."

"Jesus fucking Christ, Ben. What are you saying?"

"I'll send you money."

Meg fell against the hard mattress. Ben zipped his suitcase, stood there staring at her. Then he left without looking back. Meg gazed at the empty side of the bed for hours without moving. Recalled the day she walked into Ben's office asking for guidance. He advised her on consolidating her debts. He was comforting and warm. She made him laugh, made his extending stomach tingle. He took her for dinner, took her under his wing, convinced her to cut her losses. She was young and broke. He was old and lonely. He proposed. Bought a young woman he didn't know what to do with.

Samson hammered at the door. She dragged herself down the stairs and opened it. He asked Meg what she had done.

"What do you mean, what did I do? What the hell did you do?"

He stood face to face with his mentor's abandoned wife and warded off his own tears. He was devastated. Ben was helping him get back in the game, setting him up to be strong, to learn how to sustain his finances, and then he left. Just remain on your feet, son, he had said to Samson, you'll make a great husband. Samson didn't understand exactly what he meant at the time. Just listened to the words and the guidance his father had gone to his grave without uttering.

"Would you like a drink?" asked Meg.

Samson declined. He held out his hand, which after a moment she grabbed. Samson told her that he was so sorry. Then he backed away from Meg and loped down the driveway, getting smaller by the moment. Meg closed the door of the old stone house.

She sat at the kitchen table, poured a glass of wine. It was early but it didn't matter. She took a few sips then got up, removed the sheets from the bed, washed them, cleaned the house, scrubbed every inch of it. Then she placed a cowboy hat on her head and went to the barn. The horses were hungry so she threw them some oats and saddled Tex while he ate. The still cool sun beat through the stall windows. The animals' breath filled the barn, warming it and her. Small comfort. They cared. Even the hens cared. The goat stood on its hind legs, bleating, and leaned against the fence. The dog remained at her heels. She took a lunge line and attached it to Coco's bridle, led the horses out of the barn, and leapt onto Tex's back. What remained of the family strolled across the fields, through the orchards, rows and rows of apple trees, leaves transposed into gold.

Samson's sallow white house appeared in front of them. It had been in his family since his birth. Back then there had still been a family, and now there was only Samson. No brothers, sisters, father, mother, grandparents. All he had were the third-generation apple orchards, planted by his great-grandfather and nurtured by each father after that. Blood. Sweat. If he sells the land, then what? No family whatsoever. The roots, his roots, yanked out and burned to make way for the new wave in farming—grapes, wine.

Meg knocked on the door and let herself in. Samson entered the kitchen and smiled like he'd been expecting her, or pictured her beneath his roof all along. He organized files and shoved them into a briefcase. He was humming.

"I'm all alone," she said.

"On the contrary."

She gazed out the window at the horses, then back at Samson who was busying himself with his papers and looking very pleased. She resigned herself to moving on, to making the best of the situation. Ben promised he'd wire her money and for that she was grateful. Even though she knew it was his way of dealing with the guilt. She considered refusing it, but there she was in the country, two horses she adored and a dog with more heart than a husband. She walked toward the door, then stopped.

"Samson, people will always need apples."

"I'm tired of them."

He leaned against the polished table he'd made and asked her how she could marry a man that would leave her like that.

"What?" she asked. "How come you never married, Samson? Don't tell me you never met anyone. Around here people marry young, don't they? And if they don't marry young, they marry regardless."

He walked to the refrigerator and pulled out a pie. He placed it on the counter and returned to the table, poured two glasses of rum, plunked a slice of apple in each and handed one to Meg.

"Drink it," he said. "It's good for you."

She stared at his ageless eyes and realized that they revealed little about him.

"How come you never had children?" he asked.

"Don't answer a question with a question, Samson. Didn't your mother teach you that?"

"My mother didn't get a chance to teach me anything."

Meg glanced at the pie. The horses strolled past the kitchen window. They were tired of waiting. Horses harboured as much expectation as dogs. Saddle them up, lope through the orchards and up the road, something must still be about to happen. Samson had his lot in life and who was she to mess with it?

"Don't sell the farm," she said. "I know, I know—what do I know? What I *do* know—and learned the hard way—is not to do anything for money. Money people do things for money."

He stared at her, at her aching blue eyes, black hair, slender body. He was jealous when Ben left his house and went home to her.

"Why did you bring all the animals?" he asked.

"To entice you."

"Animals don't entice me."

Meg downed the rum, left the apple. Samson would do what Samson had to do and she didn't care anymore. Her husband had created a bond with the damn farmer that angered her from the beginning. She had to salvage her own crop. The dog howled when she walked out the door. The horses stared at her empty hands. She forgot the carrots, something she always gave them to show appreciation for their patience. Samson didn't wave goodbye. They sauntered through the orchards. The horses smelled the barren trees.

At home she threw a three-hour log on the fire, flicked through old papers left in Ben's desk. Scrambled through every drawer and unopened box for clues, letters from a French woman, photographs, condoms, anything to make sense of the secrecy. She imagined Ben standing in front of her, eyes glued to his Blackberry saying, *Okay, honey, you've got a couple of horses, a few hens, and a house completely isolated from humans. That's what you've always wanted, right? Good, good, my work is done, au revoir.* The map, all she could think of was that map of France, and Samson. What did they talk about for hours in Samson's half-lit kitchen? Fruit? Love? The fucking Sorbonne?

She grabbed her hair, wet from tears, from sweat. The dog hid under the kitchen table. She stared at the phone but didn't want to reach out to the friends she'd left. What would she tell them? *The old man you all told me not to marry accepted a job in France and left me with a tractor and a neighbour I don't know how to handle.* Rain trickled down. She locked the door, grabbed a blanket and sat by the fire recounting the day she and Ben had moved in.

She jumped when Samson appeared at the window. He held up a six-pack of beer. She wiped the tears from her face, took a few breaths in an attempt to compose herself before letting him in.

"What do you want, Samson?"

"I want to talk," he said.

"Great."

"I'm uprooting the apple trees, making space for the grape vines."

Meg thudded her head with the heel of her hand.

"I'm happy for you," she said.

The dog came and sat at Meg's feet. He knew she ached.

"I'm keeping my home, the land, adapting to the changing trends. I wrote to Ben to thank him but I didn't apologize for my feelings—quite the opposite. A foolish man deserves to be in Paris."

"You wrote to Ben?"

She ran for a pen and paper, waved them in front of Samson. She would write to Ben and tell him she didn't want his stinking money, his charity. She'd demand a divorce, break all ties with the bastard. She was young. She'd bounce back. She'd been bouncing back for months. The days were getting longer, temperatures rising. The horses were pounding their hooves in their stalls. The cock was courting the hens. She planned to plant a vegetable garden on the sunny side of the house. She was ready to get her hands dirty, work her own land. Samson held his head down. She wanted to hit it, hit it hard, then hold it against her pounding heart.

She stomped across the hardwood floors then slammed the pen and paper at Samson's socked feet.

"You took off your shoes," she said.

"I was raised that way."

"Ben never took his shoes off in the house."

She handed Samson a beer. His eyes glistened but she knew he didn't like beer. Something else was making him happy. She walked to the cupboard and pulled out the forty of Jamaican dark rum she'd bought for his visits. Why make him do anything he didn't want? He placed his hand on Meg's shoulder. She rested her head on his chest.

# Animal

MY BROTHER CYRIL calls me from JFK. Moments away from moving to San Francisco he wants to make contact. He always calls when he's on his way somewhere, which he states immediately so he has a reason to abort the conversation if it's not going his way. His springy voice, youthful and full of excitement, makes me think he's remorseless. I suspect he's not alone. He's too funny, well rehearsed. He has an audience, probably a young female, too young to care that he's an ass.

"How was Junior when you left?" I ask.

"Good, good, he'll be fine."

"And you, how are you? Was it hard saying goodbye?"

"It's not like I haven't done this before."

Over the loud speaker his flight is announced. I wish him luck and picture his beautiful estranged wife and their three-year-old son with his throaty Brooklyn accent staring out the window of their third storey condo in a newly renovated brownstone.

In my dreams a naked bald man, back hunched and arms held high, tiptoes across my backyard. I wake up. No one's standing over me. The sun attempts to get up. I beat it. Don my Kodiaks, pale blue wool hat and scarf, the only one my mother didn't make, pull on my black down jacket and grab my eighty pound husky. He's been talking since I walked into the kitchen, a medley of vibratos, howls, and whines. We may have had the same dream.

I don't know if it's right to escape to the wilderness every time I can't deal with something. My search for coyotes and deer is taking me further and further into the woods and a native friend expressed alarm when I asked if I should stop searching for wild animals. Why do you want to stop searching, she questioned. Because I'll find them, I said.

The last few days there's only been a few cracking branches in the woods but the crows went berserk and a gang of blue jays swarmed the area warning us or warning something else. Last week I saw a furry creature hiding behind a tree. My father said, are you sure it wasn't a hairy pervert? His humour that time didn't amuse me. I'm on a different plane when I'm out there. I take it all very seriously. My dog and I backed off and turned away. When we did the thing went crashing through the trees. When we revisited the area there was blood on the ice.

It's been three months since Cyril left. He didn't call at Christmas, New Year's. His two grown girls from the first marriage he left came to visit and broke my heart. They aren't drug addicts, pregnant, or drinkers despite him. But they hurt.

The cruise ship in my dreams sank and somehow everyone swam safely to shore. I did the butterfly in the opposite direction. In an attempt to lure coyotes, I've been placing my dog's poop on the border of what I believe is a pack's territory, though I've seen no sign of urine markings in the melting snow. I read this practice in a book. A woman on the same search as me placed her dog's poop next to coyote scat. Nothing happened. But I thought my case might be different. It took the entire book for her to catch a glimpse of one, and though the narrative was very appealing and sucked me in, I prayed a goddamn coyote would show up somewhere in the first fifty pages. Page 180, from a distance, one loped across an open field.

Cyril called, woke me up without apology. I was cold. I had planned that the next time he called I'd lay into him, tell him what I really feel about his behaviour. Leaving two wives, three children, hurting his good parents, his sister. His first wife says there are various types of narcissist. He seems to be all of them. My mother tells me he was never nice to me when I was young. After all these years, she tells me this while I'm pouring olive oil into the food processor attempting to find solace in the creation of a classic tapenade.

I ask Cyril how the weather is in San Francisco. He says he's not in San Francisco, he's in Utah at the Sundance Film Festival. He has a meeting in fifteen minutes with Robert Downey Jr. He's attempting to get him to appear at his film festival and he's brought along a mutual actor friend to seal the deal. He's temperamental, says Cyril. Who? I ask. Robert Downey Jr., he says. Then sniffs and says he has to go.

Since moving to the country I've spotted four coyotes, six deer, a fox and a bald opossum that looked like a baby pig. Which of all things scared me the most. We came face to face in my backyard. It reared onto its hind legs and squealed like a hyena. The dog backed away. Christ, I thought. The creature scurried under the fence.

My brother sends me newspaper clippings of his successful film festival. My sister-in-law calls in tears. My nephew won't eat without his daddy. I don my Kodiaks, yellow rain coat and hat. Raise the sleeping dog and make my way through the overgrown woods. I prod a new pile of coyote scat with a stick. There are no bones, lots of coarse hair and a few berries. In the mud, the dog sniffs the surrounding paw prints.

My mother calls in a panic. Her pastry won't turn crumb-like. She's averse to failing in the kitchen. A coyote will show itself if it wants to be seen. We don't talk about Cyril anymore, as a rule.

# The Last Monsoon

BALDING PIGEONS SHIVER on the rooftops of abandoned buildings. Their fallen feathers stick to the newly tarred street. The Mayor stares at the spectacle through his office window, scratches his head. He untangled miles of red tape to sink money into revamping the city centre and the pigeons are ruining everything.

From his desk drawer he removes a bottle of cheap whisky. His belly hangs over his belt buckle. His throat hurts. He pours the gold liquid that smells like gasoline into a stained glass. The liquid numbs his pain. He gazes at the photograph on the pale grey wall that used to be a periwinkle blue. Six men stand in a row, holding golf clubs, wearing the same red shirts. The Mayor remembers bogeying the shot that won them the tournament. They all had hair then. He chuckles at their full heads then drops his, bare and aching. Two of those men drowned in the last monsoon. The golf course was swallowed.

Clara pokes her head through the half-open door. Her skin has lost its morning lustre. The Mayor remains in the same position he's been in for hours, worrying; whisky and sweat ooze from his pores.

"Maybe you should go home and get some rest, sir. The weather isn't going to change sitting here stewing over it."

"I didn't think pigeons shed this time of year."

"Pigeons make a mess one way or the other. It's their way."

"I should have asked them to leave."

"Pigeons are unreasonable at the best of times, even more so when ill. By their very nature they're stubborn and inconsiderate. Have you ever heard of anyone attempting to reason with a pigeon?" She laughs, attempts to make the Mayor laugh. He's usually so practical. Who asks pigeons to leave? Pigeons hang out, they migrate to town squares, city centres, vacuum crumbs left by lunching blue-collar workers. Then they excrete their findings on benches, roads, sidewalks, people's heads and start all over again.

"They're ill?" asks the Mayor.

"Something's wreaking havoc on them, sir. They're thin, patchy."

"We'll have to begin again."

"What do you mean?"

"Clara, it's essential this weekend's festival is a huge success. My life depends on it. They have to go."

Clara's shoulders twitch. She squeezes her moist hands.

"Don't worry," says the Mayor.

She gazes out the window at the new clock tower, the

freshly seeded grass and the dried flowers stuffed in the hanging pots. The Mayor flips through the phone book. She backs away and draws the door closed, puts on her coat and grabs her rain hat. Outside the air moves softly, sways small branches on spindly trees and the tips of the feathers embedded in the tar. The naked pigeons coo, their dry eyes half-closed.

Clara runs her hand through her damp hair, puts on her hat. Overweight clouds swarm the distant sky. The darkening blue is smooth and silent. She walks down jilted streets, past unlit homes. Rose bushes hang flowerless and limp in grassless front yards. Porches lean. Streetlights flicker and buzz.

Candles shine through her mother-in-law's living room windows. She suspects that her husband Gene will be in the backyard devising a way to salvage the behemoths he's nurtured since spring. His hobby turned obsessive a few weeks into their marriage when an innocent experiment proved to be profitable. His first giant pumpkin grew to four hundred and fifty pounds, took eight locals and a sow to heave it to the inaugural Giant Pumpkin Weigh-Off in the square. One of an array of festivities and events the Mayor devised in an attempt to unite the community after the devastation of the last monsoon.

Growing giant pumpkins had been an aside for the average gardener. Gene's dwarfed the others, earned him a thousand dollars and his picture in the paper. Since then it has become a major event; tough, tough competition. An eight hundred pound specimen has been entered in the upcoming weigh-off. Clara refuses to divulge too many details to Gene but felt hinting wouldn't hurt. She's rarely seen her husband since.

Amidst the smell of firewood, piano music sifts through her mother-in-law's front hallway. Temperatures have been rising, yet Mrs. Lee must feel chilled. Dampness infiltrates a brick home's walls and creeps into aging bones worse than a deep freeze.

Clara enters the living room. Mrs. Lee sits on the floral up-holstered couch watching flames rage behind wrought iron. She's grinning. Her eyes sparkle.

"Mrs. Lee? You okay, honey?"

"It's on its way," she says.

"I know, I know."

Clara removes her coat and throws it over the back of a threadbare chair. It blows out a candle. Gene's mother stopped turning on lights the day the last monsoon took her husband's life. The handyman that he was thought he'd safe-proof the house prior to the storm. He sealed cracks in walls, spaces in the window panes and secured wires. Hail stones crashed against the windows. The kitchen light bulb flickered. The rain hammered the roof, the garden, the sloping driveway. Mrs. Lee huddled around the fire. Mr. Lee grabbed the step ladder from the pantry, stepped up on the rickety old metal thing. He unscrewed the warm light bulb he'd only just turned on and proceeded to screw in the new one. The force of the winds and the flood waters broke down the kitchen door; rain water rushed in and pooled around the step ladder. He flashed an eye at the light switch, watched the new bulb attempt to light the room, spark, and he was stuck. A zapping sound and the smell of something other than firewood lured Mrs. Lee to the kitchen. When a moment of lightning brightened the room, she found her husband, singed, mouth wide open.

"Where's Gene?" asks Mrs. Lee.

"I guess he's out back with the pumpkin?"

"Can't wait to make pie."

"There'll be no pie, Mrs. Lee."

"All right, all right, I'll settle for the goddamn seeds."

"You can't eat the seeds. We've been through this."

Mrs. Lee stares at the flames, hands clenched on her lap, hair perfectly preened. Clara's tired of explaining to the dwindling lady that the pumpkins are inedible, even the seeds, and Mrs. Lee loves pumpkin seeds. Everyone loves the seeds. Too many chemicals contaminate the pumpkin's innards. The stakes have changed. Enriching soil with horse and cow manure, chicken manure sparingly and only in the fall, nitrogen, phosphorous, potassium, calcium, magnesium was natural and right but far from the serious competitor's agenda.

Gene injects numerous pesticides, steroids, and a variety of chemicals into the growing fruit. They're for show, big business, like many of the larger tomatoes, watermelons and oranges that decorate the streets during the seasonal festivals.

"I hope God drowns those bastards."

"Mrs. Lee, Gene would be devastated."

"I'd love some orange juice, Clara."

"Oh, Mrs. Lee, we can't drink the juice of oranges anymore. We've been over this."

Clara makes her way to the kitchen where she pours bottled water into a rusting tea kettle and lights the gas stove. The red flag Gene attached to a pole at the top of the shed sways in the wind. Moisture gathers along the windowsills. The kitchen smells of feline urine and over-kept cut flowers. Clara bites her lip. Gene put up the flag to monitor the progress of the storm. Gentle movement was a sign, but not yet threatening. In the window she notices her hair beginning to frizz.

Beyond her reflection she catches sight of a familiar figure. She wraps her cardigan around her thin frame and makes her way through the muddy pumpkin patch. Obscured by overflowing faded orange folds, Gene strokes the side of his monstrous pumpkin. Clara clutches her chest and shakes her head. Mud cakes Gene's face. His denim jeans, plaid shirt, black hair, are all brown. The trenches surrounding the pumpkins are swimming pool deep, deeper than graves, deeper than the ravished yards from the last monsoon. He flashes the whites of his eyes at Clara.

"Not now," he says, "not now."

"When Gene? When's a good time to say hello?"

"Come on Clara, one more day, one more day. Tomorrow

this baby will take the city by storm and we'll catch up all the way to the bank."

She nods and backs away. If the storm doesn't take the city by storm, she whispers, but her husband's deafened by the brewing wind, by his own obsession.

She struggles back to the house, grabs the door knob then lets it go. She stares at her mother-in-law's house. The one they've lived in since marrying. She longs for a place of her own. Gene won't leave his mother, his crop. She ambles down the road. The insides of her nose burn. A drop of rain falls on her cheek. She stops. It's too soon. Her throat tickles. Gene watches his prize pumpkin sink with the moist air. A few drops of rain fall on his cold face. He throws himself over the pumpkin, struggles to cover every inch of it, attempts to push it and it won't budge. A few more hours, he can taste the money, the victory. He calls for his wife. Screams her name at the top of his polluted lungs, coughs, then grasps his chest. The rain soaks his too-long hair. Atop the barn the red flag beats the air, snaps in his ears. Dogs yelp. Cats run for cover. In his mother's kitchen, the lights come on. Clara strides back toward the office to occupy herself with last minute preparations. In her gut she hopes the Mayor will still be there. She needs the company.

The office is lit and empty. The Mayor stands in the centre of the square staring at the drooping pigeons. "You gotta go," he says. "I'm so sorry but you've left me no choice. I've got a festival going on this weekend proves to bring me thousands in tourist dollars, put our name back on the map and this place has got to be spotless. I don't know what's got into your systems but I'm figuring the alternative might bring you some relief and we all want to feel good now, don't we?"

He sits down on the wrought-iron bench beside the newly erected clock tower and buries his head in his hands. Two headlights turn the corner, the thunder of the heavy engine alerts the pigeons to an impending doom and before they can open their bony wings a green mist envelops the square. The Mayor runs with his lapel wrapped around his nose and mouth into his office building, right past Clara and stops.

"What the hell are you doing here?"

"Are you okay?" she asks. "You smell funny."

He slips into his office, behind the desk. He reaches for his whisky bottle; tears stream down his red, bloated face. The lump in his throat swells. It sickens him to have to hurt those birds, to hurt anything. He's a victim of circumstance, yearning for the last hurrah. The Giant Pumpkin Weigh-Off is a day away. The storm's approaching quicker than anticipated. Weather stations are out of touch. They've lost control. The show must go on. He pictures the laughter, the mouths aghast at the sight of the pumpkins. He can hear the compliments, on the square, the improvements. He imagines the people nodding and milling about with a sense of pride and hope. Clara pokes her head through the half-closed door.

"Sir, there's a green mist floating past the streetlights. It doesn't look natural."

Her pale skin's paler. She's sweaty and short of breath. Her stomach aches. The Mayor grapples for another drop of alcohol. He has to sustain composure, can't leap to his feet and grab a full, unopened bottle and pour it into his glass, slug on it and begin to lie, make up a story about the contaminants. Those pigeons, the epidemic, the pigeon epidemic, how they would have wiped out the whole town had he not taken the bull by the horns and saved the people.

Clara sits down in the antique chair at the back of his office, the one the previous Mayor's mother gave to him, a haunting reminder of his predecessor, of his predecessor and his goddamn mother. He loves birds, loves animals in general. Clara gets up and grabs a fresh bottle of whisky from his cluttered bookshelf. She pours the gold liquid into a mug and pours it down her scratchy throat.

"I'm sorry, Clara," says the Mayor. "I'm so sorry."

She pours more whisky into the mug and notices a longing on the Mayor's face. She gets up and fills his glass. He emits warmth and she can't figure out where the hell that warmth's coming from.

"Sir, my husband's raising a thousand pound pumpkin, his mother's giddy awaiting the next monsoon. She wants to be with her deceased husband. She'll stop at nothing to ensure it happens. I'm gathering by the green mist that you have wiped

out the entire pigeon population in our once-vibrant down-
town and I'm grasping for a reason why. I have to be honest, sir,
I don't believe in raising giant fruit. The whole practice is sick.
I think the goddamn seeds and all the chemicals floating in the
goddamn air were killing those pigeons. Those friggin' mam-
moth pumpkins are destroying everything; the birds, my marriage, everything."

"Clara, please. It's not true. This is politics. We do what we
have to do."

"Oh yeah, and what if the monsoon comes early and wipes
out the festival?"

"Then I'm finished, Clara. All washed up."

"You can't control the weather?"

The Mayor shakes his head, downs his whisky.

"Those pigeons died in vain, sir."

"We all die in vain, Clara."

Beads of rain stipple the square's repaved streets. The
rooftops of abandoned buildings remain empty. No sign of life.
The distant clouds arrive prematurely and rumble over head.
From his office window the Mayor watches the posters for the
Giant Pumpkin Weigh-Off float toward the drains where
they'll stick and clog and create more flooding. Clara wanders
outside. Her hat takes flight and lands in a puddle at the side
of the clock tower. She kneels to grasp it. Two tiny feathers
drift between her fingers; the cooing barely muffled by the
wind. The nest neatly tucked under the number six is safe, pro-

tected from the elements, the negligence. She spins around, watches the light go out in the Mayor's office. The wind rocks streetlights. Tomorrow, they'll begin again.

# Scimitar

I WAKE UP at three a.m., wet with sweat. The dream continues moving behind my eyes. One of large, rotting cruise ships in a decrepit, smoky harbour, overrun with faceless tourists and souvenir shops. A city I thought I knew but had no clue how to navigate. Each step weighed down by confusion and the oversized construction boots swallowing my feet. I swing my sticky legs over the edge of the bed, touch my toes upon the hardwood floor and wander to the bathroom with my hands held out to guide me.

A cool shower brings me solace in the empty hours of a new day, cleanses me of the purging my body and subconscious subject me to. I wrap myself in the bathrobe that used to belong to the man I loved and then I call Isabelle, a friend I've known since birth but never feel that close to. She rarely sleeps, so I'm not worried about the time.

"The last few nights I've been waking up drenched in sweat," I tell her.

"It's hot out there," she says.

"Not that kind of sweat, it's more serious. Perhaps it's menopause, a menopause sweat," I tell her.

"No," she laughs. "You're too pretty to be going through menopause."

"Oh," I say.

She doesn't talk long, says she has too much to do. In the mirror I study my face. It's not so pretty. I could easily be going through the change. One of many I've experienced since turning forty; wrinkles on my chest, under my chin, divots in my cheeks, fleshiness around my once-taut midriff. I tap my real nails on the linoleum counter I'm thinking of refurbishing and consider the implications of menopause. Brittle bones, hot flashes, mood swings. My lips purse. I'm accustomed to those things. I've never drunk milk. I break bones. I've been moody since ten and the sweating, although it's excessive, hasn't caused me too much strife beyond the inconvenience of losing sleep and showering at three in the morning. The phone rings. It's Isabelle.

"I've been online," she says. "You could be experiencing perimenopause, a pre-menopause. I looked at a recent photo of the two of us and you have aged, you have, it could be time."

I tap my fingers on the jade leather recliner I've considered ditching for something more streamlined and modern.

"Don't tell me these things," I say.

"You're the one who called me at three a.m. to ask me why you're sweating. So I help and this, this is the goddamn thanks I get?"

She doesn't hang up and I wish she would because I don't know what to say. I can't get the cruise ships out of my head, the bruised monsters emitting purple smoke from rusted chimneys. The water they sit in is thick and brown and I'm swimming inches from the dock. I don't look happy. I have a too-tight perm, brassy highlights and appear to be struggling not to get that hair wet.

"I have to go," I say. "I appreciate the research you've done."

I bite my real nails and wonder why I never cut her off, years ago, pre-pubescent, pre-menstrual, pre-historic. Our mothers were not close. I didn't continue the friendship to please her, or my older brother who fell for all my prettier and more endearing pals. I make coffee, although I never drink coffee. Fill it with cream so I can inundate my system with calcium by using the richest dairy product there is.

The streetlights remain dark. I'm cold. A good sign. I reach for a book, but Doris Lessing is the last thing I need and I only took one book out of the library this week for fear I'd be charged late fees on the ones I was determined to read but wouldn't finish.

I despise email but find myself clicking on the computer to check it. I had spared it from my home computer until my employer's newly created work-share program required I do my job from home three days a week and email became a necessity. Averse to members of his department working out of his sight, his smell, his auricular barrier, my manager emails incessantly.

He is everywhere. In the empty hours of morning, the shrill of the modem pierces my ears. A sound I find invasive, beyond my scheme of things. I am not titillated by technology.

Flanked by a red exclamation mark is an email from Isabelle. I tap my raw fingertips on the spacebar and contemplate deleting the message without reading it. It doesn't emit comfort, support, or empathy but I am entering the hour of self-destruction. I'm exhausted, dizzy, shaky from the new caffeine. I reach over to my cabinet, grab a rock glass and the forty of Glenfiddich left by the same man who owned the robe. I fill the glass, take a long slow sip and click on Isabelle's message.

It says, *I told you that you should have had children before he left.* Something like a bullet flies through those words and I grab my raw chest. It's a weak attempt at malice. She always wanted the men I had. Gradually, the apartment lights up with the coming of daylight. Through the dew-speckled window my past gazes back at me. I'm thinner, smoother, standing at the altar with the man I loved. Truth is we never married or intended to but I think that if I'd insinuated a desire to bond for life he wouldn't have walked out on me in the end. It must be the flu, just the flu. It's not too late to give birth, to strengthen my bones, have painless, moist sex.

I call work and tell my boss I'm ill, rundown, been up all night with a fever, hallucinations. There's a lot going around he says and there is, there always, always is. With this I believe that my symptoms are not leading to something permanent. My boss is uncharacteristically sympathetic. I don't get paid for sick days and I wish, I wish his sentiments had come from his heart and not his budgetary limitations. He tells me not to worry, to take my time, but if I get a chance to check my emails he'd appreciate it. Before he hangs up I ask if he thinks I'm doing a good job, in general, is he happy with my overall performance. Then I cry, because there's nothing else to do at that point in our conversation. After the pause he tells me I'm a fine employee.

I lie down and gaze at the ornate bedroom ceiling I'm thinking of painting pale blue. My lower back aches and I'm hungry but I can't keep my eyes open. I'm warm but not perspiring. A tepid breeze blows through the open window knocking a photograph of the man I loved onto the pillow next to me. I fall asleep with my head on his lap. I dream I'm on a rickety bus driving through a barren, concrete town. The buildings have doors but no windows and it looks like I've bought a shack in the midst of them. Doors off hinges, cupboards, rooms full of antiquated furniture, threadbare and dusty. The basement appears to have been an old grocery store. Rotted and mouldy buns remain in bins by wilted celery and stinking eggs. All the same colour. I wake up in a burning sweat, my sheets soaking, hair stuck to my throbbing forehead. Why would I buy a house like that? The sun's retreating. I've slept away the day. I'm not ready for the darkness, the end of things. I head for the shower where I stand facing the cracking drywall I need to tile.

I phone Isabelle and tell her I can't close my eyes for fear of the dreams. She laughs and says she only closes her eyes *for* the dreams.

"Let's meet for drinks," she says.

"I can't," I say. "I can't leave the apartment. I never want to leave this apartment."

"It's just a dream," she says. "I'm sure a lot of women going through perimenopause have crazy dreams."

I pace back and forth across the uncarpeted living room floor that I intend on polishing and out of desperation I ask her to come over. I have no one else to turn to. She hems and haws and says it's Friday night. A night she's been working all week for and she has no hope of picking up wealthy businessmen in my living room.

"You can't pick them up in bars either, Isabelle," I say, "So what's the loss?"

She guffaws, hangs up and arrives an hour later with flowers and a six-pack of beer tucked under each arm.

"What's the occasion?" I ask.

"It's exciting," she says, "this new phase of your life. The man leaves, one door closes, another one opens and closes. Soon you'll be unable to bear children. You'll resign yourself to your present situation, work harder at your job and being alone won't matter so much anymore."

"Jesus," I say.

She opens a beer and downs it in two gulps, then she opens another and throws the cap across the kitchen.

"Fuck," she says. "I'm so down."

"You're down?"

She puts her head in her hands and shakes it and shakes it. Then reaches her fists to the living room ceiling I've been meaning to wash for weeks. She shakes them at the cobwebs, beyond the cobwebs.

"Why?" she squeals, "Why?"

She grabs another beer, offers me one. I can't drink beer when I'm depressed. I drink it when I'm happy, angry, or at sporting events. My present state of mind calls for scotch, so I can achieve the calm one must feel before driving themselves into a brick wall, or off a cliff in a picturesque coastal town, like Big Sur. Isabelle piles beer after beer into the fridge. I don't want to tell her she's aged, that she's aged more than I. The fridge light illuminates the lines around her eyes, her mouth, the divots in the side of her cheeks, deeper and longer than mine. I don't remember her being so thin, so sharp. Her hair, once shiny black, hangs heavy and dull off her skull.

"It's okay to be alone," I tell her.

"Do you think that's my problem?"

"I don't know."

She shoves a bottle of beer into my hand and paces up and down the living room. I flip through my CDs. Search desperately for the Velvet Underground, Leonard Cohen, Son Volt, the Cocteau Twins, anything that might sedate her, cause her to recline in my distressed leather couch that I bought at an estate sale for less than a chair.

"Sit down," I say, "you're making me nervous."

"I'm pregnant."

"You are not."

"I am."

"You're drinking."

"I'm going to abort."

"What?"

She crumples onto the couch, almost in tears. I can't imagine her pregnant, even the thought of it. Not only because she's never had a serious relationship, sleeps around, hops from job to job but she lacks empathy, kindness, maternal instinct. She had no hope of ever amounting to anything, especially a mother. She never shows up in my dreams, never, in all the years I've known her, she's never been there, only when she needs me.

"Why are you in your pajamas?" she asks.

I can't believe she asked me why I'm wearing my pajamas. I asked her over to keep me company in my time of need. I'm in my pajamas because I'm ill. I've hit the wall. I'm drowning in my own sweat. My regrets are seeping into my dreams and taking me into worlds I can only assume are waiting for me on the other side. Grey rotting ships, thrumming driverless traffic, streets that don't lead to other streets, bridgeless waterways and circular train tracks that I always get stuck at when I'm in a hurry, decrepit homes and the bad hair and the shoes, always somebody else's fucking shoes on my disfigured feet. I don't want to remind her that I had asked her over because I needed someone to talk to. To determine why I can't get out of bed, can't work. That I'm sweating through everything, going under. She's beat me to the punch. I don't know if it's intentional, coincidental. Must be a bit of everything. Some women are like that.

"I'm getting fat," she says.

"At some point in our lives we all get fat," I say. "I'm thinking of getting fat myself."

"Why on earth do you want to get fat?"

"So I don't have to do anything. My work-share partner is so fat that her thin, middle-aged neighbour cuts her grass, rakes her leaves, cleans her eavestrough. I see her in Tim Hortons eating Timbits and bagels. He's raking and cutting as she eats and eats and eats. She has a fine job, nice house, good car and she eats and eats and eats and eats and eats and eats while someone else does her dirty work."

"Maybe she has a thyroid problem."

"This is the future, Isabelle. People are fat because they are immobile and eat too much of the wrong shit. People are fat because they want to be."

She leaps to her feet and walks back and forth pounding

her stomach with her fourth beer bottle. She's not glowing like other women in her condition and she is not fat, or close to it. She's thinner than I've ever seen her and I've heard of pregnant women who don't want their babies starving for two. Isabelle doesn't stop pacing, she doesn't stop and I can't imagine what kind of a mother she'll make. It doesn't make sense to me. I thought she'd be seedless, not the type of woman who should or could reproduce. But something in this satisfies me because I'm drinking the beer.

"Why don't you ask me who it is?" she asks.

"Who?"

"The father."

"The father or the man who got you pregnant?"

She grabs her purse and walks toward the door. I want to tell her I didn't go to work today because I'll never experience everything I wanted that she got without trying. I want more than a well-organized pantry, a flawless apartment. I'm tired of redecorating and spending hours labeling and re-organizing my spices by colours so that they coordinate on the shelf. The garden I've erected on the balcony is over-cared for and I trans-planted perennials from one pot to another for the first time this year in order to have even more plant babies to nurture. It was a risk, I know, and too early but everything's early these days—the tulips, the hostas, daylight savings time and the change in me.

"It's your ex," says Isabelle and slams the door.

I'm so hot I open the freezer and stick my head in it. It freezes my conscience. My heart lurches. I remove my head, close the freezer door and run to my computer. My boss has sent me five emails. I think of Isabelle, of the one thing she has and will always have over me and I don't have the heart to tell her that the man I loved, my ex, is impotent.

# Kid Airplane

GEM STARES AT the traffic light, wipes her sweating forehead with her shirtsleeve as the light turns green, yellow, red, green, yellow, red, green. Her heart thumps. She checks her watch. She's meeting a man that hits people for a living. The photos she's been studying show a large nose, broken more than a dozen times, swollen, disfigured. She makes her way into the coffee shop, orders a black coffee and sits at a table in the corner. Every man that walks through the door has a large nose and scans the room like they are looking for someone. In her purse, Gem carries a travel-size bottle of Grand Marnier, pours a drop of the orange liquid into her coffee cup resting on her lap beneath the table. She figures that he will smell the booze on her breath mixed with the bitterness of coffee but if he fails to like her for who she is, fuck him.

A stocky, tanned man with a smile on his face approaches the table.

"Gem?" he asks.

She nods, quickly sips the coffee. It blankets the nerves prickling beneath her thin skin, warms her throat.

"You're handsome," she says.

"So are you," he says. He removes his coat.

He's smaller than she imagined; twitches, sniffs. His eyes are steady. He never looks down. Gem thinks that if she were to look under the table his feet would be dancing around under there. Yet the stillness of his upper body defies that notion.

"Are you ever afraid to fight?" she asks.

"No," he says. "It's a mental thing."

"Oh," she says.

"Were you afraid to meet me?" he asks.

She hesitates. A minute ago, she would have been honest, told him, "Fuck yeah; I froze at the traffic light, sweat through my new shirt. Contemplated turning around." She smiles, drops her head, tells him, "Of course not."

Without taking his eyes off hers he nods and flicks his neck to the left then to the right. She reaches for her coffee and he moves backwards, then relaxes when he realizes it wasn't a punch she was throwing. He cracks his thick neck. Two young women look at him as they pass and whisper to each other.

Gem sips her coffee. The Grand Marnier loosens her thoughts. He sniffs, stares at her. She tries to avoid his eyes, looks behind him.

"Never look away," he says, flicks the side of his nose with his thumb, jostles in his chair, and laughs. He taps his thick, nicked fingers on the tabletop, takes a sip of his green tea. The sun streams through the window. His eyes are like marbles, green marbles with brown flecks. They're not empty like some people's eyes.

Gem contemplates his temper, wonders if he has a bad one, if in between bouts, there's a lot of pent-up frustration. She thought he'd be taller. She read he was a lightweight, but didn't think lightweight meant short.

"Does it hurt?" she asks.

"Only when you get hit in the side."

"Of the head?"

"The body: kidneys, spleen, liver. When you get hit in the head, it's like the lights go out for a second, you don't feel anything."

A guy in track pants and a blue T-shirt comes up to him and shakes his hand, pats him on the back, then walks away smiling. He's famous, Gem likes that. She asks what she should call him.

"The Kid," he says.

"I know that, but I mean another name?"

"Airplane, Kid Airplane."

He swings his neck to the left, sniffs. She imagines taking him to family gatherings, the look on her father's face when she arrives with the champion lightweight boxer, Kid Airplane. All these years he's been waiting for his daughter to hook up with someone and she hooks up with a star, an athlete. He'll be over the moon. Her sisters will seethe. Their overweight lawyer husbands will finally take a back seat at the dinner table, the fireplace. Everyone will gather around the Kid asking him to tell them about his greatest fights, the time he was knocked unconscious but came back to win the championship in the fifth round with a broken nose and eyes sealed shut with blood. Her dad will wink at her across the dinner table and flash the thumbs-up and her mother will blush when the Kid tells her how much he loves her peach pie; that he rarely eats pie when in training and he's always in training.

Gem finishes her coffee. Fluffs up her hair, looks around to see if anyone else has noticed that the Kid's out with a lady friend. She wishes she wore her low cut black blouse, pencil skirt and high heels. The Kid watches her. He smiles, almost looks away.

"I'm happy, you know," says Gem. "I'm not here because I need to be."

The Kid swallows, rubs his hands together, and flicks his head from side to side. Gem's feet dance beneath the table. He didn't feel strange, like she'd just met him.

"You seem pensive," says the Kid. "What are you thinking? Lay it on me. I can take it."

"That I'm a lot taller than you."

"There's nothing we can do about that."

"You're right."

"I used to date a jockey," he says.

"Was she miniscule?"

"No, not in that jockey way, just in a petite female way."

"What's the difference?"

"She didn't look odd."

Gem frowns. The Kid flicks the side of his nose with his thumb, leans closer to Gem and whispers, "While fighting for a space along the rail in the final stretch of a big race her right leg was crushed when she got too close to another horse. She managed to hang on for a few feet then spilled off of her mount and was pummelled to death by the pounding hooves of the other horses."

He leans back against his chair. They just met. Gem doesn't want to hear about his exes.

"Would you have married her?"

"No."

"Why?"

"She was never home."

"Doesn't your career keep you away from home?"

"Not anymore. I just retired."

"No!"

He's handsome and she likes being around him, even though he's twitchy and sniffs a lot—"retired" changes everything. If she brings the retired boxer around for dinner it won't have the same impact. Her sisters will dismiss him. Her father will ask, "What the hell is he going to do now?" Then he'll make that clicking noise with his mouth and her mother will roll her eyes and shrug her shoulders. She won't make pie. Gem checks her watch. It's feeding time. The plants need to be watered, the fish fed, the dog walked. She doesn't have time for an unemployed man in her life. She stands up. The Kid stands up.

"I want to walk you home," he says.

She wonders how he knows that she lives close by, walking distance. She looks around the room. Makes eye contact with two women having a coffee. They sneer and look away. Look at me, she says with her eyes, remember what I'm wearing: green jacket, black pants, floral shirt; my hair is short, dirty blonde. I have round gold-rimmed glasses. I'm about 5'8", 130 lbs, and my ears are not pierced. I have a scar above my top lip from falling against a sharp object when I was young. Remember me, so that when I go missing you can tell the police that you saw me with a short, stocky bald man with a black jacket and a crooked nose. Tell them you think I left with that lightweight boxer you've seen on TV—Kid Airplane. She can see it now all over the papers:

> Local Woman Abducted by Newly Retired Lightweight Champion Kid Airplane; The Kid Lashes Out; Retired Boxer Loses His Mind; Out of the Ring, the Kid's a Lost Soul; Retirement's Hard on a Professional Athlete.

Her dad would be amazed. Her mother would know exactly how to field the slew of phone calls. For the first time her sisters would want to tell everyone that they are related to her, the woman in the paper.

They walk out of the coffee shop and down the road.

"I like you," says the Kid.

He stops, looks at Gem. His face, though it has been visibly battered over the years, is soft and kind. He tells her that he wants to get into politics. She nods, knows nothing about politics. They continue walking. His feet are small. She towers over him and it makes her feel strong. He stops again.

"My real name is Neil. You can call me Neil. I want you to know the real me. Neil. I am Neil, and you know, it feels really good to tell you that. Wow, thanks for sharing the first day of my new life with me."

Gem looks down at the ground, at her tattered shoes. She's glad she didn't wear heels. She senses her dog pacing around the living room, wondering where she is. She's never not there on time, never deviates from the routine. Neil looks around, sniffs. Now that she knows his real name, when he sniffs it's like he has an allergy, a cold, a nervous tick. She liked him better when he didn't seem real.

# Fuselage

I YANK QUILLS from a stray dog's nose. Despite his cries, he doesn't resist the aid. The tearing eyes and pinned-back ears say it all. In my own desperation, I appreciate being appreciated.

Before the dog arrived I'd spent the entire dark evening listening for tires on gravel. Whistles, howls, buzzing, cracking branches and the general hum of air make it difficult to discern man-made sounds. An owl shrieks and I jump; though handsome and wise, they are killers.

In his absence, my cousin Heathrow told me not to watch the stars. Said I'd go insane and if one fell it would take me with it. He spends too much time staring into space. It isn't illusions that drive me crazy—quite the opposite. A hundred moments fixated upon a non-existent entity suits me fine. If I fall, so what.

The dog drinks the entire contents of my last water bottle. I count on my cousin to bring plenty more, along with some chips, sours, smokes, and the local paper. It's frightening when all my eggs are in one basket. Memory is not his strong point.

I expect too much. At this point I could eat almost anything, although my hunger is weakening now that I have company.

"You feel better, kid?" I ask the dog.

He doesn't answer. Not even with his eyes. We barely know each other and a dog's loyalty is earned. I had relieved him of what had probably been the most painful time of his life. I could teach the dog a thing or two about suffering. To him I must not look like one who suffers. I had for the most part a healthy disposition except for my tendencies—fits of rage that come from nowhere and always end in damage, but humans are not without tendencies. Society brings them on. This dog was the first thing I'd encountered in my life that wouldn't judge me, unless of course I was cruel. I could be cruel, but not to animals.

Droplets of blood speckle the dog's nose. He doesn't have tags, appears well-fed, taken care of. A handsome dog is rarely a stray and this disturbs me. Someone would be searching for him, calling out his name. Come daylight an entire family could converge on this site and the jig would be up. If he hears their cries he might leap to his feet and run to them, leaving me hidden and he won't tell them of our rendezvous, of that I was certain. I always wanted a dog for that reason. Something to tell everything to; spill the beans, let it out, be truthful, up front, get it off my heavy chest.

"I'm going to call you Opus," I say.

The dog twitches his ears.

"Opus, it's been a long road. You've come in on the last leg. If I seem short it's because I'm exhausted, worn out."

The owl must have caught a field mouse. It's ceased communicating. Everything's ceased communicating: coyotes, raptors, mosquitoes. Still no distant rumbles, car engines. Heathrow's been gone too long. I imagine he stopped at a roadside joint for a beer. It's like him. He'd eye a girl or two then get back on course. He has to get back on course. Sunrise comes slowly until it's here.

If I take Opus, someone will be heartbroken. Losing a pet is like loosing a limb. His head rests on my thigh. His long golden coat softens my hard hands. He's going to make me regret not wanting children. I can't lose my edge. *Okay, okay,* I want to say, *I got rid of the quills, get out of here, go on, get.* He's keeping me warm. We're keeping each other warm.

Heathrow must be getting laid. It's been stressful on the road. A few times he looked at me funny and I grabbed my mother's old switchblade I stole weeks ago from the kitchen cupboard. He saw it. I knew he did when he took a long haul on his ice cold water bottle. *Even if I was the last woman on earth, asshole.* Before reaching the border he tried that look again as I reclined along the back seat attempting to sleep. The temperature must have been at least ninety degrees. Awoken by the sweat dripping off my nose into my open mouth, I brushed my damp hair off my forehead and sat up. My dirty skin appeared tanned and oiled and I felt his stare ricochet off the rearview mirror through my ragged tank top. *Stop the fucking car*, I yelled and a grin dented his face as if he believed I was about to comply. *Get out*, I screamed, *get out*. And he did. I got into the driver's seat and motored down the road until I couldn't see him anymore.

I pulled into a desolate motel with a diner and dusty outdoor seating area. I ordered a cheeseburger, fries and a pitcher of Colt 45. Heathrow traipsed up beside me disheveled and lame. I asked for an extra glass and a menu. I hate eating alone. Nothing like that happened again. I'm effectively unattractive when provoked.

Heathrow had been complaining of the journey. Homelessness is hard on a young man. In his eyes, I spied a yearning to dart when I entered convenience stores, taverns and latrines. I'd listen for tires screeching but for some reason he never left. We'd grown up together. Our mothers were sisters. Lived side by side. His separated, mine widowed. They sought solace in each other's misery. *Losing a spouse is like an amputation*, my mother said. *We're bodiless limbs.* I'd envisioned it the other way around but my mother said a woman is all arms and legs, she has to be, there's too much to do. A heart breaks and it's useless. A woman can love her children without it. Their love is in their arms. *Feel it*, she'd say, *feel it when I hold you.*

Young Heathrow threw baseballs and made me try to hit them. He stuck toads in hoses and waited for me to howl with him when they blasted to their demise. He laughed but rarely spoke. Always looked over his shoulder. I'd look too but never saw anything. *What are you looking for Heathrow?* I'd ask. He'd stare at me. I don't know if he didn't want me to know or I should have known. We each bore insensitivities.

My mother always held me. I never questioned her bodiless love but always wondered why she didn't succumb to our doctor's advances. He was middle-aged, a widower himself. I could have loved him like a father, and if not that deep, a good uncle. The type I'd heard about but didn't have. Either way he would have made me feel secure and I wanted to see my mother looked after. He went out of his way to bring a smile to her face. He brought a smile to her face but he never made her blush. Heathrow's mother didn't like him, wouldn't look him in the eye. I overheard this one night when the doctor asked my mother what her sister had against him. He knew her husband had been cruel and loud but argued that he was his own man. That she shouldn't condemn all men on the grounds that she married a bad one. The only male she'd look in the eye was her son and Heathrow always looked away. In school I learned that most predators, dogs, wolves, raptors, rapists, perceived eye contact as a threat. All I knew was the doctor shouldn't take it personally because my aunt wouldn't look at the mailman, the milkman or the handsome plumber either. I remember Heathrow's dad was large and yelled a lot but I was young when he was shackled and dragged away.

I imagined that I'd be happy alone in the woods, and now with a large golden dog on my lap, it was a done deal. I wondered if I'd be sad if Heathrow never came back. That, in some way, it would liberate us once and for all from each other, from our mothers, our fathers, the stinking old past. I could take the dog without remorse because I'd be good to it. At that moment in the temporarily still night I was ready to love something. I don't know how it happened, but it happened and I couldn't bear the thought of losing the feeling. The worst part about a missing pet was worrying that whoever took it was not kind to it. But they can rest assured, that family, I will love their dog, love it more than I've ever loved anything, more than my long-gone father, even my mother, my tough and loving mother.

Heathrow didn't like dogs. He didn't like anything vulnerable and dependent. He had scars. I promised him a good life, that I would lead him to safety, to a place where he'd never have to look over his shoulder. Somewhere even ghosts wouldn't find. Society never brought us much hope. I could live without it. Heathrow might need a woman on occasion but I would be fine with Opus.

Opus licks my hand. I know he's grateful. Finally, a car engine, the flicker of headlights. I'm not relieved. I was ready to make a go of it. Since treating Opus, I hadn't watched the stars but why else would my eyes be seeing little glimpses of red flashing through the dark trees. I must have been focusing on something bright to create such oddities in my vision. The trampling of branches like a herd of buffalo, a trick of the mind. The trumpeting of low voices, a delusion. Flashlights bring Opus and I to our feet.

It didn't occur to me that a policeman would pick up Heathrow at a gas station, his arms full of water, potato chips, licorice and cokes. I know he didn't mean to lead him to me. He attempted to say I'd run off. It didn't occur to me that before Opus had a run-in with the porcupine he'd been sent into the woods alongside two hounds and a German shepherd with explicit instructions to locate Heathrow and I. It didn't occur to me that I had done anything wrong. I'd simply done as I was told.

Heathrow's father had been released from prison a few days before he travelled by foot to the neighbourhood we'd relocated to. It might have been a vibration, an instinct screaming in my gut but I knew a dark force was nearing. I spied him from the living room window, lurking in front of the houses. He was taller than I'd remembered, which is unusual because as a child everything seems bigger. On the inside, he must have kept on growing. His anger grew and it showed in his fists, his black eyes. I ran to the kitchen and pulled a chair over to the pantry where I stood on it and scrounged around for the shoebox I knew my mother kept on the top shelf.

Not long after Heathrow's father was taken away she sat us down and explained if he ever came back to grab the gun from the box. *We have to get him before he gets us*, she said. Then she winked and nodded her small head. She took us into the woods, covered our ears and taught us how to shoot. *A man like that doesn't come back to patch things up,* she said, *he comes back to take us all to hell.* We were scared, but I was excited about learning to shoot guns. Heathrow wept. He maintained a belief that his father would return to patch things up.

Heathrow's mother and my mother were sipping mint juleps in the backyard. I know because I'd picked the mint, poured the bourbon over ice, added the sugar, following my mother's exact instructions. I carried the full pitcher outside to the giggling ladies enjoying a sunny summer afternoon with their feet up and sun hats protecting their already weathered faces. Heathrow sat with his legs crossed at the end of the yard, sucking on a long piece of grass, staring at the sky. He had no ambition.

Our houses were side by side without anyone else around us. It was odd that it worked that way. The geography of the area was meant for unbalance. It was laden with trees and lilac, at one time a railroad town. But the station had been closed for years, the tracks overgrown and the homes scattered in their original places like seeds that sprung from one main tree in no particular pattern or order. Our mothers appreciated the solitude, that we were obscured by the once-was. For Heathrow and me it was too isolated and I resented that we had to hide to stay alive.

My uncle's shadow stretched across the sunny grass. Sometimes the body acts before the mind or maybe it's the mind acting before the motor functions twig to the fact they're being moved. In tandem the shadow and I raised our right arms, the left arms followed, grasped onto the right wrists, chins lowered, eyes focused. I watched our mothers slowly turning around and Heathrow leapt to his gangly legs. In a moment I would have watched them all die and although I was fearful of pulling the trigger, I could never let my mother down. I'd made a promise. He turned around and spotted me and I hated him. I hated the bastard for plaguing every single moment of our lives with and without him. I felt the stampede of rage make its way through my veins, every morsel of my young but aging body. There are times when one heralds the tendencies, relies on the mania. I burst through the back door.

"You fucking bastard," I screamed.

As he swung around I pulled the trigger, again and again and again. He went down like a lump of coal. I dropped to my knees shaking like the ice cubes against the etched glass pitcher my father had given my mother for their 10th anniversary.

Heathrow's almost-dead father moaned as blood oozed from his head. The mother's squeals pierced my ears. They were entangled in each other's limbs. Those arms and legs that kept us together, the arms that loved me like nothing else. And I fired over and over and over again into the heart of the bleeding man.

Heathrow stopped me. I grabbed his arm and ran, ran into the front, into the old car that always had the keys in the ignition and money in the glove compartment and I drove and I drove and I drove. If my mother represented the limbs of our unit then I was the body. I embodied my mother, my aunt, my cousin. I did it for them, slayed the dragon, liberated the mothers of all burdens. It was time the kids began a life of their own.

The policeman touches my shoulders, attempts to lift me up by my armpits. I hear the crackling radio in the background and Heathrow sniffling. I cling to Opus and pray we'll meet again.

# Tourniquet

LADY SITS ON the garden chair, grabs her script and begins to study her lines. She accepted the role of Mrs. Julia Gibbs in the community theatre's production of *Our Town*. She's been grappling with doing her part for the community, felt an obligation being the town doctor's wife. All the other wives do honorable things, volunteer in schools and run charity auctions. Before marrying Gabe she'd been acting in films mostly, small budget productions with little to no distribution. She studied theatre, believed it's where real actors honed their craft. Was lured onto the screen by a need to feed herself. When Gabe proposed, she was ready for a change. The prospect of being a wife excited her. She'd never been one before. Despite Gabe's desire for her to keep it up, she relinquished her acting career for domesticity and a part-time job teaching drama to school children. She found teaching rewarding, told the mothers that kids are good actors. They dig deep, feel and fear everything and it shows on their faces which is great for the stage.

Gabe leans on one of the ancient trees that remain in the back yard, trunks like the skins of alligators. He takes a few deep breaths and rubs his forehead. Lady senses him. She rubs her back, her tight shoulders. They've been aching for weeks. Her husband told her that her muscles were so hard if he threw himself against them it would kill him. Gabe stares at his wife.

"What do you think trees do all day?" he asks her.

"What?" she says. "I don't know. Sway in the wind? Hang out."

He rolls his eyes. They've been rolling for weeks, every time she walks into the room or answers one of his pointed questions the wrong way.

"There's more to *them* than meets the eye," he says.

Lady gazes down at her purple and green hands—the veins stick out when she's nervous, nervous or hot. She's not hot, despite the blazing sun, the breezeless morning. Gabe fills the watering can, speaks lovingly to his plants as he showers them in rain water. Lady rubs her hands. She wonders if there's no more to her than meets the eye. Surely he hasn't excavated her entirety. She's convinced that every ten years she's new. The yogi who lives down the road told her that other people's behaviour mirrors one's own. She watches her husband in an attempt to understand herself. She sees nothing familiar, not a single gesture, a twinkle in the eye, a giggle. Lady gets up and joins her husband by the garden he planted when they bought the house and has nurtured like a child for over ten years. She confesses she can't imagine life without him. He pats her hand and focuses on the weeping willow languishing by the river.

"I don't relate to trees, Gabe, okay? Not like animals. I have an affinity with animals. I like the way trees look but I don't sympathize with them."

He shakes his head. She waits for a response. He gazes at her.

"Oh, I recognize the hard work they do, don't get me wrong, some are beautiful, hauntingly beautiful, huge, enigmatic but they're not human, honey."

"Neither are animals, Lady. I love trees," he says. "I love them."

"This is about the old maple I had chopped down out front, isn't it?" she asks.

"Yes, Lady, it is."

He trims the white rose bush and nicks his finger on a thorn. He shoves the finger into his mouth. His eyes fill with tears. She places her hand on his back and he steps away. She can't count how many people commented on the chopping down of the maple. In the bank, the grocery store, mothers of her students. "Poor, poor tree," they said, shaking their heads, condemning her for her ruthless decision. *Poor tree?* she thought. *My God, all those leaves, its roots infesting and plugging the sewer pipes, the flooding of the basement, it was a pain in the ass.* She begged the city to cut it down.

"Are you really that upset about it?" she asks her husband.

He removes the flaccid finger from his mouth.

"I cried, Lady. It's very sad. You killed my favourite tree."

He applies pressure to his bleeding finger, walks away from his wife. Lady looks around. Birds turn their back on her and gaze into the neighbour's yard. A menacing breeze arrives from nowhere, rustles the other trees' leaves. Lady stares at her shrinking feet, a symbol of her waning identity. She hadn't asked her husband if he cared about the destruction of the tree, how he was in general? He never asks anything of her and in that she assumes he's okay, then she chops down what matters.

She returns to her garden chair, picks up her script. Imagines how Mrs. Julia Gibbs would handle the situation. She was a great wife. Knew all the right things to say and do. It was the fifties. Life was temperate then. She slams her unmemorized lines on the garden table, strolls to the river and sits on the bank. She used to worry that if she had children one might disappear from view, run down to the river and drown.

Purple and yellow wildflowers and a few willow trees line the river bank. Birds flitter amongst the age-old trees that are doing far more than meets the eye. Gabe moves back to his garden chair. He coughs, makes his presence known. Lady knows he's watching her. She wonders what she can do to make it up to him. She can't bring back the tree or erase the sides of her that have surfaced through their union and pretend they don't really exist. She's sorry that she doesn't rally for the preservation of all things natural and pertinent to a healthy world. The wolves and falcons she'd fight for, the salvation of the Arctic, poor thin polar bears, for the animals she'd strike. Teetering on the river bank, Lady realizes there's nothing natural about her. She's an actress and no matter how hard she tries, she can't seem to change that.

Gabe walks to the front yard. She senses his departure and follows him. He looms over the bare spot that used to be occupied by the maple. They were told the city would be back to cover the space with sod. The gaping hole amidst the well-manicured lawn doesn't bother Lady as much as her husband's pain. It's just a tree, honey, she wants to say but there's no such thing as just anything in his world and what amazes Lady about marriage is how those individual worlds identify themselves more than ever.

"I can't bring it back." she says. "What the hell am I supposed to do?"

Gabe walks away and disappears into the studio above the garage that was originally constructed for Lady to practice her lines, breathing and role playing. Her stomach aches but not from hunger—from loneliness. She reaches inside the front door, grabs her purse and car keys and drives into town. She heads to Tony's diner, orders a piping hot tea. It soothes her insides. A mother of one of her drama students walks by and tells her she's so excited about the upcoming play. The woman's cheeks blush and it makes Lady anxious. She yearned to act again but *Our Town* wasn't doing it for her. She asked the director why they insisted on choosing the production that every community theatre or high school stages outside of *Oklahoma*. She introduced them to Tennessee Williams, Arthur Miller, Eugene O'Neill and Edward Albee but they stuck with *Our Town*. "It's safe," said the director, "you know, ordinary." But Lady knew there was nothing safe or ordinary about Thornton Wilder.

The waiter watches her from the counter. She detests being watched when she's out of character. No matter where a woman goes, there's always someone watching. She finishes the tea, pays and leaves. In her car she pictures Gabe's face. She drives to the pet store. Aquariums gurgle. Bright yellow, blue and red fish gaze at Lady. A grey-haired woman draped in a flowery smock, hair tied back in a bun appears from behind the counter. On her shoulder rests a long furry creature with bulging, wet eyes.

"Welcome," she says. "This is Sebastian. He's half price today. No tax."

"I'm not partial to rats," says Lady.

"He's a ferret."

"I was in the market for something a little more common," she says. "Like a kitten or a fish."

When she got married, Lady wanted a puppy. Her mother swore by having a dog in a marriage for back-up. They decided to wait until they were settled. They were hoping for children.

"Fish?" says the shopkeeper. "This is the goddess fish. It buries beneath the sand and swims sideways. Beautiful, isn't it?"

"I once played a fish in a small movie I made after graduating," says Lady.

The shopkeeper looks at her, places the ferret in a cage.

"It was a surreal indie film. I didn't have to wear a fish costume or anything. It was alluded to . . . that I was fish. I learned a lot about myself in that part. I had to reach, really reach to achieve my motivation."

The shopkeeper softens her voice and tilts her head sideways.

"Is it for yourself, ma'am? Are you in need of a pet, something to keep you company, to talk to?"

Lady looks around the place. Takes a step back. "No, actually, I had my husband's favourite tree hacked down to salvage the pipes, stop the flooding and lighten my autumn chores. He hasn't been the same since. I've created a hole in his life. I didn't realize one could get so attached to trees."

"Oh, yes," she says, "there's more to them than meets the eye."

Lady scratches her head, feels every fish's eyes on her. The ferret turns away. She can't move, wonders if she should go home and pretend that she's a tree. It was one of the first exercises she learned in theatre school, to be a tree. She'll go home and stand in the yard with her arms held high, wrists limp, and emit oxygen, give the birds a place to nest in, then there will most certainly be more to her than meets the eye.

"Do you think I'm just an idiot," she asks the shopkeeper. "That you have me all figured out by taking one look at me?"

The shopkeeper shrugs; the ferret twitches its nose. It smells.

In the car, Lady sits and watches the empty sidewalk, the closed up shops, the For Sale and For Lease signs posted in dusty windows of abandoned buildings. She spots a poster for the upcoming play on a decaying telephone pole. The wind blows a grocery store flyer across the windshield. It sticks. She gazes down at the rings on her finger. Remembers how she twiddled them everyday for months after she was married. She wanted desperately to be a good wife. She pretends she's Mrs. Gibbs. Mrs. Gibbs wouldn't cry at that moment. She'd look at the bright side. She'd carry on.

The nursery is located a few minutes from home and although Lady doesn't feel like being that close to home, she makes her way to the nursery. The air is fresh, the sun hot, the breeze cool, a perfect balance. In a few weeks the leaves will fall and she'll be holed up in a cozy house wondering why she's not dreaming of the roles she didn't get and her reluctance to achieve stardom. It was never the reason behind becoming an actress; she genuinely wanted to know what it was like being other people. She did it for herself and when it ceased to amaze her, she was happy to move on.

She knows a few filmmakers who promise to put her in their next film but she's shied away from their proposals blaming it on her withering looks and that she's teetering on middle-age. Despite Gabe's encouragement, Lady believes that to be on the big screen a face needs character, if not beauty, and she's at that in-between stage. It's an awkward time for an actress. She steps into the nursery, pictures Gabe handing her roses after the screenings of her little films.

"I need a sapling," she says to a woman with dirty hands and a sun burnt face.

"Any kind?"

"Are they all called saplings? I don't know. It's a baby maple I'm after."

"I have an oak."

"How many years will it take to grow to a substantial size?"

"You're the one who had the classic maple cut down from the Pearson's old place, aren't you? You're the one who changed the landscape."

Lady's vision grows fuzzy, the woman in front of her has two out-of-focus red heads. All the blood freezes in her veins and though the counter didn't get higher, she must be shrinking because the two-headed woman towers over her. If she could move, run, she would. But she knows she'll be back in the spring for annuals, and topsoil and running won't accomplish anything. Running never accomplishes anything.

She lugs the baby tree to the car and places it in the back

seat, drives along the barren road. The sky tumbles above her. A saloon song wavers from the radio, velvet vocals lamenting about land being like a wild goose and painting a different colour on a front door. She pulls up her driveway and sits in the car for a while. Perhaps she should have bought a dog. She needs something to leap out and greet her happily. It's been so long since anything was happy to see her.

A voice whispers in her ear and she knows it's Mrs. Gibbs. She can't escape her. Next to being a real wife, portraying the perfect wife is the hardest part she ever played. Gone are the days when she was almost always cast as drug addicts. Mainly because she was waifish, sallow-skinned and moody. She never did drugs, was a diligent student of the Stanislavsky method and used every aspect of her otherwise addictive personality to fill the roles. She believed that if she'd found a drug she liked she'd have been a really good addict. They were easy roles to play, effortless. Lady closes her eyes, allows herself to slip into character.

She removes the oak from the back seat of the hot car. It appears thirsty, what few leaves it has droop. She swears she can hear it drinking as she douses it in the rain water that gathers in a barrel at the side of the house. She wraps the gold ribbon she bought from the nursery around the baby tree and places it on the grassless spot where the maple lived for, she was told, at least sixty years. She didn't feel like a murderer up until that moment and as Gabe walks out of the house smiling, something wet trickles down her face. She's crying without making herself cry.

# Mandible

ARNOLD CAST THE line into the river. Perched himself on the edge and gazed at the still water. Henry rolled his blood-shot eyes and slid into his garden chair. He'd grown impatient over the years, couldn't take the early morning dampness or the necessity to remain quiet.

"My bones are stiffening," he said.

Arnold moved his head without diverting his eyes from the line.

"Muscles stiffen, Henry. Bones buckle, lock and break."

"They're aching, asshole. The dampness is killing me. It hurts, everything hurts."

Arnold stared at the ripples in the water and jumped to his feet. He'd been waiting for the big catch. If he persevered, and he had persevered, good things would come.

"My time has come, Henry."

"Don't tell me, tell the fish."

Henry tensed his aching muscles. Remembered the day Arnold and him met at the creek in the back of the run-down suburb they called home. They caught tadpoles, kept them in jars and watched them sprout legs. Henry spent most of his youth around bodies of water. He was in awe of all things that lived beneath their surface. He no longer kept anything he caught. Those days were over. He fished on Sundays for Arnold, a way of placating his lifelong friend. It didn't take much to spend a few hours with an old friend to help him think it was never too late to catch the fish of his dreams, as long as he threw them back in.

Henry pulled a crossword from the knapsack, reached into the cooler and grabbed a bottle of cold beer. Arnold forbade cans. They made more noise when opened. Henry peered over his newly acquired bifocals and wondered if Arnold was happy. It would be unfair to ask him until he asked himself. Are you happy, Henry? Really happy? Are you really, really happy, Henry? He used to be happy at the end of a fishing rod but that was a long time ago, before marriage, children, and the indifference toward his sport. He'd been a pro, was born with an affinity for fish, always wanted to be a fisherman. He was the best in his field. An overabundance of trophies weighted down the household shelves, the mantelpiece and windowsills, along with newspaper clippings, rows of video. He'd competed in over a thousand tournaments and made as many public appearances.

One morning, a cool breeze blew from the south. He cast his line and the *wsssh* didn't move him. He yearned for his couch, the TV, a six-pack, chips of any kind and nothing more.

Heaviness tugged the line, bent the rod. His teammates yelled at him, "Reel the damn thing in Henry, reel it in," but he couldn't. He couldn't stand the thought of staring into the eyes of another desperate fish. "No more," he yelled, "No fucking more." He dove into the water and swam to shore. His coach reeled in the twenty-pound pike. Its rubbery eyes gleamed in the rising sunlight. Henry kept walking, walked until his feet ached and the sun burned the top of his pounding skull. On his way to the couch, the fridge, when he gazes at his trophies, he has no clue what happened to the man who won them.

"Do you know, Arnold, that when the Chinese get old they head into the depths of the country to be at one with nature."

"What are you talking about, Henry?"

"I don't know why because nature's fucking frightening and it'll only let you in so far."

"Not now, Henry. Sshh."

Henry watched the turkey vultures swoop overhead, wasting the day surfing the wind tunnels; tattered, lumbering wings jaded the perfect sky. What a life, he thought. He'd spent twenty years searching for meaning in the wilderness, spent hours attempting to relate to fish, only to learn that he could never be one of them. Shadows loomed above him. He kept turning around, peering up to the edge of the gorge.

Arnold never questioned Henry's relationship with fish. Even though at times he thought he was a little too close to them. Figured he talked to them because that's what fishermen do, like a race car driver talks to his car or a jockey his horse. His wife constantly made comments like the fish get far more attention than his boys, or her. He watched his buddy sip on his beer, tap his pen on the newspaper. His weathered skin added twenty years to the man he'd followed like a puppy, a good mother, supportive, loyal, excited by every one of his accomplishments, from the largest pike to the trickiest rock bass to the walleyes that he caught. He was always there.

Arnold's fishing rod rested in his hands. Nothing tugged at it. The flow of the water was the only thing moving it. The bait swayed with the undertow. He mulled over Henry's words. He'd changed since retiring from his sport. Lost a sense of balance, rarely slept. His wife called Arnold regularly, begging for help, some remedy that could help her get through to her husband now that he'd resigned himself to sitting in the dark, watching television, drinking beer, rarely talking. He says he's haunted by guilt, she told Arnold. Something about all the lives he's taken. Henry told Arnold he had a recurring dream about a fish with teeth like chainsaws gnawing at him slowly until he apologizes, apologizes for killing his brothers. Arnold felt something tug on the line, didn't get his hopes up in case it was a weed.

"They know we're here, Arnold."

"So what are you saying?"

"Arnold they're as opportunist as the next being, have a fucking beer, make some noise. It doesn't make a goddamn difference. You hook one, you hook one. You think the damn thing gives itself up for nothing."

"I think you need help, Henry."

Henry stared at the crossword. Mulled over the clues. If he didn't get a word instantly he moved on to the next one. He stared back at Arnold and wondered how he'd ever had the patience to fish. He was twenty when he turned pro. Up every day by two a.m., drove hours in the dark to tranquil lakes, boarded boats before sunrise and waited quietly over and over again for the bite on the line. A chill surged through his fingertips. He looked up and over his shoulder.

"Arnie, I'm all washed up. Where did I go wrong?"

"Come on, Henry, grab your rod, you'll feel better once you get your line wet. Just sitting there's going to get you down."

"I'll let you in on a secret, pal, there's no reason to get up early, the bastards leap around all day. If they're hungry, they'll eat. Don't over-analyze a fish, man, and never ever get attached to them."

Arnold had enough. He'd envied his friend for years. He lived his dream, was a professional fisherman. A success. A celebrity. He didn't realize how lucky he'd been and Arnold was sick of his whining, the apathy. If that's what happens to a man who's lucky enough to accomplish his dreams, thought Arnold, got everything he ever wanted, nice cars, the girl, two smart kids, attention, loads and loads of attention, what a disappointment. If you spoil a dog, it turns on you. If you spoil a kid, it turns on you. You spoil a grown man, he turns on himself.

"I think you should leave, Henry."

"Why?"

"Because you're giving off negative vibes. The fish sense it."

"You know I didn't like catching those fish, Arn. I loved fish. I did what I did to be with them the only way I knew how."

"I need to be alone, Henry."

"You can't do this without me, Arn. I taught you everything you know."

"That's a lie, Henry, and you know it. That could have been me and you know it."

"You made your bed, Arnold. You can't blame me for that."

"Go to hell, Henry. Go to hell."

Henry rose and walked to the crooked steps that wound from the foot of the river to the top of the gorge. So many times he'd leapt down those steps excited, thrilled to begin his day with his orange neon bait whisking into the tumbling waters. It was so good then. He trudged up the steps scattered with leaves, each thigh contracting, sending needles through the under-worked muscles. Seagulls' squeals filtered into the gorge with the frigid morning air, bristling the hair on Henry's neck. He looked back down at Arnold. He was quiet, still, waiting. He yelled down to him.

"You're not going to catch anything today, Arn."

"You are wrong. I sense a big catch. A big catch."

"Yeah? Ever had a big catch, Arn? A really big catch. Huge brother, huge. One so enormous you have to get help to reel the bastard in, tail thrashing, eyes bulging, fucking mandibles yearning to chomp your jugular. Baby, that's a catch, the kind of catch you better pray you've got backup for because that sucker's gonna eat every last bit of you if you're not prepared. Are you prepared for that, Arn? Are you? Preparation is everything."

"Christ, Henry, what's got into you? You think I'm here to hook a shark?"

"I don't know, man. I don't know."

At the top of the stairs Henry studied the chaotic mess of fallen tree trunks. In the distance, he saw a creature leaping. It must be a deer, he thought, attempting to disappear before daylight. But it didn't look like a deer. He removed his toque, scratched his sweating head. He listened to the breeze, to the cracking of branches, the squawking of greedy birds. His heart pounded in his chest. He could hear the breeze, the river rushing, his own breathing. Arnold's voice startled him.

"Henry, I've got something!" he yelled. "Henry, Jesus, I've got something on the line."

Henry stared at the tips of his boots, wiggled his numb toes. His circulation hadn't been the same since he fell into freezing water, overzealous about a catch that never amounted to anything. Arnold's howls for aid rung through his over-sensitive ears. "Quiet, Arnold, it'll let go," whispered Henry. "You scream like that, it's going to unclench its jaws and you'll have nothing. All that energy, that emotion, wasted. There'll be nothing at the end of the line. You're the one who said it, Arn. You've got to shut up. Shut up, Arnold, shut up."

Henry's head spun. He lost his footing, fell to his knees, grabbed a fading elm that hadn't been strong since the last frost. He teetered with it. Above him the light blue sky spun in circles.

"Henry, Henry!" cried Arnold.

Henry meandered to the edge of the gorge and stared down the rocky shore. He fixated on the small bald man bracing himself against a tree attempting to reel in a bending rod. Henry focused on his old friend's red face and white knuckles. He screamed for Henry, screamed over and over again. Henry fixated on the tumbling rapids, the bare sky. A sharp breeze blew across the back of his neck. He brushed away the sensation. He didn't want to feel it. It was too much to take.

"Henry!" screeched Arnold. "Henry, help me, for God sake! Henry, please. Please."

"Okay, Arnold, I'll help you." He teetered on the edge of the cliff they used to leap off as kids. He stared at the still water, envisioned a school of fish lurking beneath the thick green surface, swimming in circles, taunting him. He took a deep breath, more breath than his shrinking lungs could handle, raised his arms to a peak in front of him, leapt onto his toes and thrust himself away from the rock wall. He opened his eyes, welcomed the feeling of falling, of letting go, letting everything go. He was the fishing rod, the line being cast into the water, the bait.

# Over Dinner

IN THE BANGKOK GARDEN, the faux river murmurs at the foot of a fig tree. My mother looks pretty in pale blue cashmere. Her eyes sparkle beneath the asian chandelier. The river rests behind her. Four manchu lions glide from one end to the other. They are fancy for goldfish. On the outside, rivers are always moving. Those fish wouldn't see the same vine twice. My mother's elegant fingers grasp her virgin mango cocktail. She speaks of William Least Heat-Moon; he says *the river is death waiting*. Onto our table the waiter places sea bass wrapped in banana leaf, cuts off its tail. The goldfish scurry behind the fountain.

My mother recalls a television show about Native hockey players, a particular boy's struggle. He couldn't hack the injustice at hockey camp, went AWOL, hopped the bus home and entered the kitchen. At the stove, his mother wouldn't turn around. Her son's footsteps gave away more than they should have. His mother's back, the coldest reception. The brick wall he'd keep on running into. Anything worth having is surrounded by obstacles.

All he wanted was acceptance. All they ever wanted was acceptance, young Native boys on skates, dreaming of the big leagues, to be just like the other boys, to be like everybody else. He picked up his bags and got back on the bus. The river is death waiting, even when frozen.

The waiter fills my glass with Thai beer. A goldfish grazes the surface.

"Was he successful?" I ask.

My mother nods.

"What did his mother think?"

"She was right and proud. A mother only wants what's best for her child."

The lemongrass paste tingles my palate. Three goldfish mill around the lily pads. I comment on the tranquility of water. The waiter brings hot towels and Jasmine tea. We cleanse our hands.

My mother revisits William Least Heat-Moon. She says, "In *River Horse* he wrote: *The ocean is the wind made visible and the river is the land made liquid.*"

The goldfish flutter in succession. I touch her peaceful hand. She tells me that the hockey player is Ted Nolan. He overcame the odds, made a name for himself in the NHL. The waiter produces the cheque. I ponder the distance in my mother's eyes. She's a million miles away from the wintry Canadian city, in Bangkok, by the river, embracing what matters in life.

# Sweet Tea

MAGGIE POURS COLD black tea into the Mason jars we bought at the kitchen shop on the corner of Union and 7th. She adds sugar, bourbon, a slice of lemon, mint and a red polka-dot straw. She hands me the drink. I take a much needed sip and step onto the fire escape. Below me a man kisses a short plump woman. It isn't the first time I've been privy to such tenderness from this location. The man has a perfectly round bald spot on the top of his otherwise hairy head. He's extremely tall. I wonder if the woman has known him long enough to have run her hand across it, spied it while he's sitting or lying down. They walk away from each other. He turns around. She doesn't. I watch for the slender, dark-haired guy to walk past with his husky. Every day at five, they walk by. He wears well-worn T-shirts, Converse, shorts to the knees (khakis mostly), and sunglasses. Maggie pokes her head through the open window.

"You should wait for him on the stoop," she says.

"What? I don't want to meet him. It's the dog I'm interested in. It's beautiful."

"It doesn't hurt to say hello."

"It doesn't help, Maggie. I'm better off up here."

My tongue lags on the last syllables attempting to leave my mouth. The bourbon softens everything in sequence, beginning with my head. Once I stepped outside I felt my skull folding in on itself like a soufflé that's been out of the oven too long. I sit down on a rusting step. Maggie joins me, leans on the railing and sips her tea out of the blue polka-dot straw. Her waist is tiny, her wrists childlike. When she left home she looked older. Her son yells from the other room. He's lost the guinea pig.

"Honey, he'll come back when he's hungry," she hollers.

"They're always hungry," I say.

"Exactly," she says.

Her son yells for his mother again and again. She sips her drink. The bourbon doesn't seem to be hitting her like it's hitting me. Her eyes are steady, mine splayed.

"There he is," she says.

Across the street the guy and his husky stroll past. He's wearing a red T-shirt, blue shorts to the knees, beige Converse untied at the top. The dog always looks the same, regal, well-groomed, its tongue hanging to its chest. The temperature is radioactive. The heat from the sun doesn't feel as bad as the heat rising from the asphalt. My ankles are swollen, water balloons. My belly has lost all sense of itself, hanging over my pelvis in rolls. In the morning I'm a different woman. Thinner, sleek. I can never bump into the guy and his dog after a day in the sweltering heat. Up here I'm light, celestial, watching over them like a Botticelli angel, rotund yet ethereal.

"The other day I bought water that said on the bottle that it came from clouds," I tell Maggie.

She widens her eyes, sips her drink, releases the blue polka dot straw from her newly polished teeth.

"That's absurd," she says.

"It is absurd," I say and picture the new industry, long black pipes descending from clouds, blocking the skyline, the panoramic view of mostly everything, making it hazardous to fly, to walk, to drive; the water industry sapping every last bit of moisture from the sky.


"There'll be no more rain," says Maggie. "Or sleet, or snow. How great."

I weigh the pros and cons of no precipitation. I bet Maggie's thinking of hair, her straightened curly hair. The humidity wreaks havoc on my usually bone-straight version. I work to get it how my sister's naturally began. In two hours the guests are coming for the dinner party that Maggie's throwing, a way of introducing me to her friends, to make me feel welcome. We've been baking and cooking all afternoon: chocolate cake, icing, fennel and potato salad, roasted garlic marinade for the seven-pound pork butt that's been slow cooking in the oven for six of the required eight hours. The apartment smells of chipotle, garlic, lemon, and cocoa. The guinea pig should be making its way to the kitchen any minute. Maggie's son has stopped searching—he has another one. I'm tired from cooking, the heat, walking. I hadn't been in a place that I could walk around in for years. I drive everywhere back home. The other day, I took the Q train to the end of the line, got out, found and walked south on 5th Ave until I couldn't walk anymore. I ached in places I didn't know existed. I had no recollection my legs went up that high. My ass hurt, my toes, the balls of my feet. I had shin splints.

On the train back to Maggie's, I sat next to a man who stared at the bruises on the inside of his arms. At first glance he didn't look like a junkie. You never can tell. He had messy grey hair, tons of it. I found him attractive until he drew attention to his tracks. There was a time I would have found them equally attractive. He had a Sonic Youth patch sewn onto the thigh of his jeans and a hole in the toe of his sneakers. I'd never walked around Manhattan alone. I was proud of myself, liberated. I wanted to tell the man sitting next to me with his bushel of grey hair how happy I was. He looked at the shopping bag I was holding. In an attempt to relieve him of the painful awareness of his weaknesses, I was tempted to tell him about the books I'd bought. A biography of Picasso, another book about Picasso and his dog Lump, photographs of them, his last wife Jacqueline, the disheveled La Californie and his goat named Esmeralda who slept on the villa's second floor tied to an armoire. I love goats. Picasso would have understood me. I'm convinced of it.

I sip my bourbon-drenched tea. Maggie lights a cigarette and blows smoke out of the side of her mouth. I wonder what difference that makes. She looks down and twiddles her straw.

"I'm excited about you meeting Gordon," she says.

"Who's Gordon?" I ask.

"He's this guy I play squash with."

"You play squash?"

"I took it up because I can't stand going on dates in bars and restaurants. This way we date on the squash court."

"That's smart," I say.

"Yeah, if they don't play squash, I won't hook up with them."

"I prefer not to hook up with them."

"You'll never get anywhere."

"We have different needs."

She stares at the sky. I think she's staring at the sky. She's quiet, and she's rarely quiet. I wonder if she's looking up in order to prevent the tears that are welling up in her too-blue eyes from cascading down her numb face. I love her, despite my envy. I grab the red polka-dot straw between my retracting lips. Sip my drink. Wait a few minutes for the next wave to hit me because in this recipe Maggie swears that each sip's a trip.

"Do you think it's wrong to have a crush on a goat?" I ask.

Maggie looks at me without smiling. She's still, wide-eyed.

"Yes," she says. "That's really pushing it."

The guy and the husky trudge back up the street. Maggie leaps to her feet, leans over the fire escape.

"Hey, hey," she says.

The dog looks up, stops and wags its tail. The guy follows its stare.

"We're having a dinner party tonight and we'd love you to come," yells Maggie.

He laughs. He laughs and the dog wags its tail more fervently and Maggie leans further over the railing, her left leg lifts and ankle swivels. Her shiny blonde hair and porcelain skin gleam. She must look even more beautiful to the man on the street looking up.

"You know," he says, "You're on. I'll be there. What the hell, I'm in. I'm in."

He laughs again, looks down. Maggie twiddles her hair while she tells him what apartment number we're in. He walks away laughing, the dog grabs its leash in its teeth and prances ahead of him. Maggie looks at me, rubs her hands together and crawls through the window into the kitchen. He doesn't seem like Maggie's type. I don't understand. He doesn't look like he plays squash.

I down my sweet tea. My head swirls. My stomach aches. The fire escape sways. It isn't swaying. Something's swaying. I'm in a kayak. I am a kayak. I grip the red polka-dot straw in my teeth and close my eyes. I'm not dressed. I'm not ready. I don't want to meet anybody, no one. I want to hang out here on the swaying, unswaying fire escape with my sister and talk about what the hell we're going to do with the rest of our lives. I want to watch things, just watch—people in general, men, women, the guy with the husky, the husky, its beautiful gait, coat, tail, eyes, tongue that hangs down to its chest. I don't want to know them. It'll change everything.

I crawl through the window into the kitchen. It's sweltering. The orange and black guinea pig sniffs around the foot of the fridge. Maggie throws it some fennel. It squeals. Her son runs into the kitchen, hugs his mother's legs. He has her nose, my hair colour.

"Silly piggy," he says, and runs out of the kitchen back into Maggie's office to search eBay for a specific type of watch that he wants. He's four.

"Aren't you excited?" she asks.

"No, I can't believe you did that. I'm dumbfounded."

"That's not a good way to be," she says, "especially after the tea. It's not meant to cause strife, quite the opposite. It's a Southern potion."

"I'm no stranger to your potions, Maggie. He's not coming here for me."

"In the end, he'll be here for you, doll. That's the way it's always been. All's well that ends well."

"Maggie, I don't care."

"I care."

"Then you have him. I'll take the dog."

She pours more bourbon into the half-empty jar, grips the blue polka dot straw between her over-polished, blinding teeth. The guinea pig sniffs at my toes, looks up at me and squeals. When I arrived their food bowls were barren, half-gnawed carrots dried out and turning colour lay beneath the empty water dispenser. The soiled cage smelled. I bought them food, fresh bedding, talked to them, stroked their coats. All the while they squealed, didn't take their black eyes off of me. Every time I walk into the room they run to the edges of their cage and call to me. I love being needed, responded to and accepted so genuinely. Maggie works too hard, alone in New York, raising a clever, fatherless boy. Her sense of humour, like her beauty, never falters. I wonder what she really feels like on the inside—sandy, gritty, bruised, dizzy, floating, lifeless. She's far from lifeless. She rarely sleeps, eats, so the fact that the guinea pigs need some attention isn't the big deal—Maggie needs attention, to be fed, caressed, watered, and cleaned out. She would never admit it. When we were young I was the one in need; afraid of my own voice, to step outside. She strips down to her light blue boxer shorts and bra. Her stomach is tight like a male model's. Her hips have disappeared over the years. She's tanned from a bottle but it's even and bronze. She strides across the living room; her son takes his clothes off and follows her to the bathroom. She shuts the door behind her. He runs back to the television, throws himself onto the couch and asks for some corn. I look at his little face. To tide him over, I make him a peanut butter and jelly sandwich. He's beautiful, especially when eating.

"You're a cherub," I say.

He asks what a cherub is and I begin to explain how they are heavenly, winged then I stop and simply say that a cherub is an innocent child. He gazes at me, holds his full mouth still, raises his eyebrows and I nod because, like him, I know he's far from innocent. The guinea pig ventures toward the sandwich. I grab it and it squeals. "I caught the piggy, Jay." He nods his head and points to the cage. His mother exits the bathroom and glides across the living room. Her hair has been blown straight and its silkiness glimmers in the setting sun streaming through the uncurtained window. I hope Gordon is more than a good squash player; one that's kind, a good lover and willing to help raise a son that isn't his—a really special squash player.

The smell of the pork's marinade permeates the apartment. Jay's holding out for the corn-on-the-cob only because he wants to use the multicoloured corn holders we bought at the kitchen store. He's been jabbing them into the embroidered silk cushions, awaiting the corn, the homemade chocolate cake. I don't know what to wear. Maggie comes out of the bedroom dressed in a tapered black dress and sequined flip-flops. Her lips are red. She leaps onto the couch and grabs Jay in her arms. He giggles, tells his mum he loves her. Hand in hand they rush into the kitchen to put cobs of corn into the not-yet-boiling water. Their laughter echoes through me. The guinea pigs squeal. Jay runs by with hands full of fennel then scurries back to the kitchen, picks up his yellow and red corn holders on the way. When the doorbell rings I jump. I'm not ready to meet people. I look down at my faded jeans, the ones I've worn since high school, and my Indianapolis Colts T-shirt I'd ordered online before they won the Super Bowl. I've been a fan long before the hype. I get up and press the button that opens the downstairs door and I wait, hear heavy footsteps, the creaking stairs. I run into the kitchen and stare at my sister. With the blue polka dot straw, she's stirring the brown liquid in her Mason jar, humming, conjuring up potions. The knock on the door startles me.

"It's Gordon," she says. "He's always early."

Jay runs past me. I follow him. He opens the door in the nude. A tall man in a blue suit covers his mouth with his hand, then plunks both hands onto the top of his head.

"Jay, we've got to stop meeting like this," he says.

He's funny, the man in the suit. Jay wraps his thin arms around the man's thighs. Maggie bellows from the kitchen that Jay wore his birthday suit just for him and Jay raises his arms in the air and squeals, *it's my birthday?* I can't remember the last time I saw him around someone that resembled a dad. It's amazing how even the essence of family warms a place. I introduce myself to Gordon and rush into the bedroom to don the pink dress a friend of mine lent me for the trip. I never borrow clothes but I liked the dress. I brush my frizzing hair, pull it back into a ponytail and apply mauve lipstick to my thinning lips. Through Maggie's bedroom window, I spot the guy and his husky. He's standing across the street looking up. He's smoking, running his other hand through his disheveled hair. The dog sits next to him, watching him, tail sweeping back and forth across the concrete. I shove on the Grecian-like flip-flops that Maggie gave me to wear with the dress and sneak out the door. On the way down the stairs my throat tightens. When I get to the stoop, they're gone. I cross the street, stare at the three cigarette butts lying by my shimmering violet toenails. For a Friday evening in Brooklyn, the streets are quiet. A slight breeze blows across my half-painted face. Laughter draws my eyes up to the fire escape. Maggie and Gordon are standing out there sipping sweet tea from Mason jars. He's stroking her face. Her left foot plays with his pant leg. I told her that the guy with the husky wasn't coming to dinner to meet me. I look up and down Union Street. Despite the cigarette butts, there's no trace of them. I wanted to meet the dog. I only ever wanted a chance to meet that dog.

# The Market

IN THE MARKET women in headscarves fill canvas sacks with chestnuts and sweet potatoes. A cat zips past a raving man with a broom, a fish tail dangles from its clenched teeth. I study the saffron, always thought it was yellow. It's a jewel. Expensive like gems. Something I imagine a snake charmer has stashed beneath the viper's basket. I envision red sand and beyond the sand, a golden city—flowing silks, sitars and bongos. Outside snow falls on the city I'm really in. It's been snowing for days. Huge white flakes I feel I know by now; they may be different but they all look the same to me.

I place lemons in my bag, limes, cilantro, ginger, garlic, a pomegranate, though I may never eat the pomegranate. A strange fruit, too difficult to eat, something good shouldn't be so hard to consume. I'll challenge myself with it, slice it open, place it on my kitchen table and wile away the wintry hours studying the intricacy inside. I'll hold it up to the window, a touch of red in January. My pomegranate, more than a fruit, a pastime, a hobby, a job.

Sawdust blows across the market floor as two men in pin-stripe overalls and caps lift bananas from a crate. I wait for the spiders to creep out, thick black beasts that cast shadows on basement walls. I've read about them in science magazines, how they crawl into the banana crates and hitch a ride to the land of opportunity. I half expect to take one home with me inadvertently and fall victim to its venom. I can see it now, woman dies from spider suspected to have entered the country with bananas sold in the local market. There are better ways to go— I'd rather succumb to a death with more of a ring to it.

I grab a small silver shovel and shove it into basmati rice, pour the rice into a brown paper bag, sounds like rain. The smell of roasting chestnuts fills my nose, along with the dust from the rice. A small hunchbacked woman with gold front teeth smiles and hands me a dried fig. I take it and she motions for me to put it in my mouth. I'm not partial to dried figs but I don't want to offend her so I eat it. She smiles and nods. "Yes, it's tasty," I tell her. I feel bad for lying but I doubt she understands me. She hands me another. "It's actually awful," I say and she laughs. Maybe she does understand me. I'm so presumptuous. My toes point inwards, my cheeks burn. The woman turns away and picks up knitting needles laden with green wool. That's what I get for telling the truth. She gave me a fig, a goodwill offering. I'm tired of lying, but decide I can't give it up on account of sweet old ladies in the market.

A clock the size of the moon warns me my time is running out. Roman numerals are hard to read so I pretend I have no idea what time it is, what time is. If I don't return to the office at one p.m. like I do every day, five days in a row, will the bosses notice? When the phones ring and ring and ring and ring, they'll realize I'm gone. I wonder if they'll furiously search under desks, behind filing cabinets, in washroom stalls, the elevator, stairwell, call the police. I'll be a missing person. I could go missing for days, take a vacation and not tell anybody, to Bombay, meet the snake charmer, pepper exotic dishes with saffron, kiss the nose of a hypnotized snake.

A man with shiny black hair tied back in a ponytail saunters past the spices I've been smelling. He stops at a vegetable stall, picks up potatoes, turns them around in his hand then places them back down. He steals a grape, then another, doesn't look over his shoulder, then another. The young lady manning the stall polishes apples and talks to the woman selling candles beside her. They laugh, expose their happy teeth, white as only real happiness can be: pure, untainted. Laughing and polishing apples while the tall man with the ponytail steals grapes behind her back. Someone worked their ass off to pick those. I pay for the rice, saffron, turmeric and cumin and follow the man. He strides up to the butcher. Three skinned pigs dangle from a hook. The rotund butcher has a sweaty forehead and blood on his white coat, on his gloves. He laughs with the man with the ponytail and points to a large steak, no bone, meat a deep purple. "Grade A," says the butcher. From that moment on I refuse to eat meat.

It's been a big day. This morning I swore I'd quit smoking, drinking and taking too many over-the-counter painkillers for no reason. By nightfall, I'll be a nun. "Make it two of those," the man with the ponytail says. I feel his breath on the side of my face, like he turned to look my way when he spoke. I don't look up. I head over to the fish counter and think of an alternative for dinner. I've bought everything to make chicken curry and now that I don't eat animals, I better change a few things. Shrimp, perhaps. There's something less cruel about eating a crustacean. The man with the ponytail exudes a subtle scent, a mixture of things, citrus—and grass? I wonder if he dabs it on his neck or chest, whether like me he sprays a bit of it in the air and walks through it. It's too fresh for his look.

He peruses the live lobster in the tank. He fiddles with his hair as he watches them. Is he waiting for one to speak to him, for some kind of sign, the right lobster to perfectly accompany the big steaks he bought? I could recommend a lovely wine; a nice full-bodied Bordeaux, hint of cherry, leather, well-balanced tannins, to follow with a cigar. But first a haircut. The lobster tank reflects his face, his large eyes; shorter hair would bring those eyes out, highlight his cheekbones, jaw. What a waste, all that shiny black hair pulled into a bunch at the back of his head. A snip to his chin even to thicken it up, give it some shape, bring out his handsome features. Think how much more attractive he'll be at his surf and turf dinner, sipping wine, smoking a cigar with his new hairdo.

A small man in spectacles and clogs approaches the lobster tank. Nods and shoves his hand into the water, grabs two lobsters, claws bound with elastics, eyes doomed. Their bodies droop, they've given up. I bite into the green apple I bought, resign myself to a life of fruits and vegetables, grains, beans. Poor lobsters. Why not kill them before they come to market, like the pigs dangling from the hooks. Spare them the humiliation of being hunted by humans peering into the tank, choosing their feast. Then into a boiling pot of water, squealing. I feel sick.

My cell phone rings, vibrates against my thigh. I leave it there for a minute. I turn my back on the clock and walk over to the coffee shop, grab a decaf, sprinkle cinnamon into it and chocolate. The breadmaker pulls a loaf from the wood burning stove. A group of women who work at the bank next door to my office huddle around the bread, titter to each other and pat their stomachs, thighs and asses. Their cheeks are aglow. They waft hands in front of noses, giggle. One says, "Bottle that smell." The man with the ponytail walks up behind them and grabs a baguette. The women all turn to look at him, kick and knock elbows with each other. He places the bread by the cash register and eyes the baker's other goods, pastries, tarts, éclairs. He takes his time, points to the chocolate éclairs, the cream puffs, profiteroles. The lobsters don't move in the bag they're in.

I watch for a sudden escape, nothing—stillness, silence. What about the pineapple tart, I want to say. He looks over at me. I avert my eyes to the danish. The women have moved on. Returned to their jobs. Jobs they'll have forever. I wonder if the man with the ponytail is married to a woman like that, one that drools over bread and oppresses herself from indulging in it. There are worse things not to indulge in: heroin, speed, murder. Everyone should eat fresh-baked bread. My phone rings again, vibrates against my thigh. "The pineapple tarts," I say. In the reflection in the pastry case, I look smaller than I am, squat. The man with the ponytail stands up straight but doesn't turn around. Our eyes meet in the glass. I back up and make my way through the vegetables, the fruit, the cheese and the dangling pigs. I don't feel like I'm being followed. Behind me everyone's busy sorting their goods, cutting, slicing, speaking to customers, laughing, holding up tenderloins, offering dried figs, nodding, taking money, returning change. A huge man wearing rubber gloves slams a fish head onto ice.

Yellow, all I see is yellow, unable to determine any other element to the colour enveloping my gaze, not fingertips, just yellow and then the fingertips, then the pale crust, a smell of sugar, then a waft of citrus and grass. My cell phone rings, reverberates against my thigh. It's nothing in comparison to the reverberation in my gut, around my sweating heart, my brain. These uncontrollable sensations have to be triggered by the mind, maybe the nerve endings. Fluttering feelings are all in one's head, a concoction built on emotion, attraction, fear. We are driven by illusion, goddamnit.

If I grab onto that tart, I'll lose my job. The job I've been trying to lose for weeks but haven't had the guts to walk into the boss's office and say, that's it, that's it, I'm boarding a plane east—the real East. The place where plump-bellied bronze buddhas smile all day perched upon hills surrounded by cherry blossoms, and I'll stay until snow houses are erected to enshrine the God of Water. Then I'll head for the red sand, goat-laden streets, seek the snake charmer and search for the ghosts of western architects that lost themselves there. If I grab onto that tart, I'll eat meat, drink wine, plunk the lobster into boiling water and smoke a cigar.

# Blue Parrot

CASS OPENS HER eyes when the front door closes and Mitch's size ten steel-toe boots thump down the front porch steps. She peers out the window at the back of him, at his straight brown hair resting on his shoulders. She releases the curtains and falls back against her pillow. She stares at the ceiling. Notices a crack she hadn't noticed before; something else to worry about along with the chugging furnace? If only cracks in ceilings could be read like palms. When the phone rings she buries her head under the sheets until it rings again. She answers, doesn't say hello, just, "Leave a message."

"Oh, I thought . . ."

"Oh my God, Lila."

"Hello?"

The phone falls to the floor. Cass leaps out of bed. Her head spins. She grabs the side of the dresser. Pain shoots through her stomach, into her lower back. She looks around the room at the clothes strewn everywhere, the drooping Canna lilies in the window, the dusty picture frames. "Oh, my

God," she says. She rushes into the kitchen, eyes the unwashed dinner plates, pots, pans, the pile of unopened bills on the table. She slaps her thighs, those thighs in need of stretching and walking then reclining in hot baths.

Lila knocks on the front door, rings the bell that Cass didn't even know they had. She forgot that her sister-in-law was coming to visit. They'd had a hard time remembering anything these days with Cass being under the weather, the never-ending restoration of their newly acquired Victorian house, Mitch's job at the station, the unpredictable nature of life itself—the curve balls, as Mitch liked to say, the curve balls, the spanners in the works. Everyone has their shit to deal with Mitch said one night while stroking Cass's damp hair out of her face. Whether it's the guy that shoots his ex-wife before turning the gun on himself, the newcomer from some far off fucked up place that's trying to master driving a cab on the wrong side of the road just to keep his family alive or the retired judge whose life savings got siphoned away by some hedge fund pyramid scam—how's that for justice. Everyone's got their shit to deal with, Cass, he said as his eyes closed and his head hit the pillow before he'd had a chance to remove his gun, his badge, and his steel-toe boots.

Lila shoves her cell phone into her pocket, places her bag on one of the green plastic Muskoka chairs. She runs her fingers over the peeling paint on the banister. Then she hammers on the front door again before letting herself in.

"Cass?"

Cass pulls her stiff jeans over her painful midriff, leaves the belt at the first notch. She rushes into the bathroom, reaches into the medicine cabinet and grabs a silver flask from behind the many pill bottles with her name on them that she refuses to take. Without looking in the mirror, she swigs on the Cointreau in the flask. She figures it's orange-flavoured so it's like having juice—a more potent shot of vitamin c. It's there for mornings like these when she needs to calm her nerves quickly. An exercise she swears will stop when she regains her strength and feels human again. The flask's almost empty but she doesn't count on feeling human before the liquid runs out.

Cass opens the bathroom door and peers into the living room. Lila places a long box onto the coffee table and begins unraveling the packing tape that seals it shut. She reaches into the open box and pulls out something blue.

"Lila?"

Lila spins around and smiles.

"I'm so sorry, Lila. Mitch said you were coming tomorrow." She bites her lip, silently apologizes to her husband for lying. I'm sorry, I'm sorry, honey. What else could she do? He'd have done the same thing. She holds out her arms and gives her little sister-in-law a big hug. Lila clutches Cass's sweater with her fists. Her small frame quivers. Cass leads her into the kitchen, where she grabs a box of tissues from the top of the dusty fridge.

"I'm just tired."

Cass fills the kettle. "Maybe in our next life we'll come back as men, Lila, and get a taste of the other side of life."

Lila wipes her eyes and heads back into the living room. She returns holding a blue ornament that looks like the head of a pelican. Cass realizes it's the blue parrot she bought Lila and David for their ninth wedding anniversary. Pottery is the traditional gift for the ninth year of marriage but Cass hated everything she saw and next to the local potter was a glass blower. She figured if they were both created by local artisans that glass must be akin to clay. Besides traditions are up for re-evaluation these days and it's the thought that counts anyway.

Cass entered the glass blower's studio and the blue parrot greeted her instantly. It's like it spoke to her when a glint of sunlight cascaded off the glass and she was won over by the life in its eyes. Mitch found it hideous but when offered the opportunity to go out and choose his own gift for his sister's anniversary, and he had to look for pottery, he suddenly had a change of heart. Cass prayed Lila hadn't come to visit so she could return the parrot. Where would she put it? She was surrounded by things she didn't want.

"Oh, Cass, being a man wouldn't be any different."

Cass raises her eyebrows and envisions the flask in the medicine cabinet. "You're right. You're right." She gazes out the kitchen window. "In my next life, I want to come back as the neighbour's dog."

Lila strokes the parrot's head.

"Why the neighbour's dog?"

Next door the white German shepherd reclines on the overly green grass. Its feet twitch, what looks like a slight smile stretches across its polar-bear-like face as it dreams the morning away, not a care in the world. Puttering around the garden is the man that loves it unconditionally. A love it reciprocates.

"Are you hungry, Lila? Have you had breakfast?"

Lila glances around the kitchen, scrunches up her still youthful face. She's petite and pretty, like something you'd find on top of a birthday cake. Her pink sweater fits her like a glove. Lila stares at the parrot. Cass waits for her to spill the beans about how much the damn thing has plagued her, how it doesn't fit into her perfect home's pristine décor, expensive taste and how— more importantly—it isn't pottery. That would be just like her to drive all this way to point out a thing like that. People like her thrive on making a point. But she doesn't; she draws the parrot closer, puts her ear to its beak, nods her head and looks back up at Cass, who's wetting her lips with her tongue in that way she does when she walks through a liquor store.

"Do you mind if we eat out?" asks Lila. Then she looks at the parrot and shrugs.

Cass grips the gritty counter top with her fingernails. A sharp pain shoots through her stomach, reaches down to her cold toes. Knowing that Lila's peering through her proverbial microscope the house feels cold, filthy, slanted and she knows it isn't slanted. She's been the same since they met; smiling, always smiling, while muttering her asides through clenched sparkling teeth and never having the guts to come out and say what she really thinks, always alluding to the disparagement while pretending to like her brother's choice of wife for her precious brother's sake. It's been eight years since Cass married Mitch and Lila's tongue never dulls, and now she has a sidekick— strength in numbers, even if it's one other and inanimate. What nerve she has to disrespect Cass in her own home. To have a good old tête-à-tête with the parrot right in front of her. It's a hundred times worse than when Lila used to whisper to her friends when Cass walked past them in high school. Cass grips the inside of her cheeks with her sharp teeth.

"What does the parrot have to say, Lila?"

"Oh, nothing. You know . . ."

Lila glances at the floor, the fridge, the windows, the stove, the packed sink. "Just that we'd rather eat out, that's all. We don't want you to have to go to any trouble."

Sunlight glistens through the window, meets the blue glass parrot, creating the illusion of movement, of blinking, twinkling eyes. Cass shakes her head. "Does the parrot want a cracker?"

"That's not funny."

"Oh, I apologize. Is it not that kind of parrot? You know, like a real one."

"He is real. You're just jealous. You've always been jealous of my things."

"What?"

"Remember my pony?"

"Oh, my God, Lila. I liked your pony. And it wasn't a pony it was a goddamn Hanoverian—your dad worked his ass off to buy you that horse. I wasn't jealous of you; I was in awe of the creature itself."

"Are you going to freshen up before we go out for breakfast? Do you need to take a shower, wash your hair?"

Cass's stomach burns. Not from the old pain but from the new pain Lila disperses. Family. She excuses herself and enters the bathroom, takes a swig of her special juice. She stares at her unwashed face in the toothpaste-splattered mirror. "Oh, God," she says. Then scoffs. Baudelaire summed it up for her one day when she read, *God is the only being who, in order to reign, doesn't even need to exist.* She splashes her face with cold water, plasters Oil of Olay over it, the kind that comes with a touch of foundation, one less step she has to take to look half pretty. She is pretty, it's hiding beneath a veil of a temporary melancholy.

One night when she couldn't sleep, she told Mitch that of all things, she really hopes she gets the life back in her eyes. She gazes into the mirror, sticks out her tongue. Even the damn parrot has life in its eyes. She pokes her head out the bathroom door. Lila chatters away like she's entertaining a child. The last time Cass and Mitch saw Lila she was newly pregnant and throwing herself a congratulations party. Cass and Mitch agree on the not-telling-until-after-three-months rule because things can go wrong, and they do.

The tap runs, dishes clatter. Cass slaps her forehead, another sip of juice. "Get a grip," she says. The liquid warms her throat, then a pang of pain. The pill bottles vie for attention. She doesn't want to stop feeling, can't imagine the highs without the lows. She'll deal with the anger, the regret. She'll pull her head above water in time. She simply needs to subvert the discomfort while she's awake and attempts to get things done around the house. The orange-flavoured liquid is instant. The pills are permanent so she leaves them in the bottle. She turns on the shower and tiptoes into the bedroom, picks up the phone. On Mitch's cell phone, she leaves a message to inform him that his sister's arrived and she's brought a friend. Then she sits on the edge of the bed. In the neighbour's backyard, the white Shepherd stretches across the back deck washing its legs with its ruby tongue. Mitch calls back. Cass doesn't want to stress him out with too many details, just says Lila's arrived, she hasn't changed and asks him to bring groceries and wine, lots of wine. He sighs. And sunflower seeds.

"Sunflower seeds?"

"Maybe you could take her out for dinner later while I clean the house?"

Mitch hangs up the phone. Cass runs her hand across the wainscotting the real estate agent raved about that she finds clunky and old. All she wanted was a home she could move right into and exist in with little-to-no effort and they fell in love with a house in need. The dog lurches to its feet and howls at the back door of its master's house. The sun warms the room. Cass pulls the quilt over the bed and straightens the variety of pillows she bought in different colours to brighten the place until the walls were fixed and the new paint can be applied. Everything takes so long to come to fruition, a house to a home, a family. The water ceases running. A bell rings. Children's laughter erupts in the schoolyard across the street. Cass slams the window shut, draws the curtains. A piece of plaster falls off the yet-to-be-improved ceiling. The contractors have been drywalling and priming the buckling walls for weeks. In between coffee breaks, cigarettes, and stories of their lives, they get a few hours work done then go to the tavern for beer and complain that Cass hasn't picked out all the things they need to carry on to the next step—light fixtures, paint, cupboard doors.

She runs her sleeve over a photograph of Mitch. When they first started dating, Lila used to fill Mitch's vulnerable head with ugly stories about Cass in corrupt teenage girl style to try and break them up. Cass couldn't figure out if Lila wanted Mitch to find someone more like her, or if she wanted to always have him to herself. Often he doubted Cass when she'd plead her innocence. It's taken time but now he believes his wife.

Lila stands outside the bathroom door and calls Cass. Cass rolls her eyes, looks around the room for an escape route. There's no way out. "I'm in here," she yells. Lila appears at the door. One hand holds the blue parrot close to her chest, the other clutches yellow roses.

"Who's in the shower?"

"The new me."

"Oh, nice. Well your neighbour gave us these roses to put in the guest room. She said it will make the place smell nice and add some colour. I guess you're having trouble picking paint colours?"

"She told you that?" Goddamn contractors. She knew that woman was out there probing them while they spent too much time fixed to the curb drinking coffee, smoking, and whining on her dollar. Bastards didn't really want to do the work, were tired and dirty after an hour and ready to go home, but they blamed Cass. It was Cass's fault that there was no paint and no light fixtures and no cupboards but the truth was that the walls weren't ready to be painted, lights to be hung or anything else because they were behind schedule. It's a vicious cycle, a vicious cycle and it doesn't make an ounce of difference that her husband's a cop because the cop's never around. They were unable to make it to the house for a couple of days. With Lila to contend with, it's a blessing to have a few less fingers pointing her way.

"Your neighbour's house is so lovely and spotless," says Lila. "And I see what you mean about the dog."

Cass wets her lips, fumbles with the ends of her fingers, unsure if she's going to punch herself, the wall, or Lila.

"When did you see the inside of the neighbour's house?"

"Just now when I went next door to ask them if I could borrow paper towels and dishwashing liquid—oh, and milk. You're out."

"I haven't exactly been able to shop lately, Lila."

"Hmm, it's not like you didn't know I was coming."

"I'm sorry. I . . ."

"It's okay. Some women aren't natural mothers and others aren't natural homemakers. You know, it's like we're just sup-posed to be good at both. I think it's okay to only be good at one or the other. The world has changed. Women aren't the same as they used to be. However, women like your next door neighbor, they're obviously really good at both—she's old school, eh? And she's so beautiful."

Cass's mouth drops open. Her eyes sting. She thrusts her stiff finger toward the window. A sharp pain shoots through her shoulder. She grabs the side of the bed. "Well it's easy for my next door neighbour to have kids and a perfect house—she doesn't work. She has a rich husband, a young Brazilian pool boy who disappears into the house when her husband's at work, a great dog and a laudanum habit—next door it's always a bed of fucking roses."

Lila thrusts the parrot's head under her arm and turns away. "Cass, please, not in front of Blue."

Blue? Blue? She shakes her head. Envisions white sand, aqua-marine water, can picture the tips of her toenails newly pedicured a lovely lilac draped over a beach chair. Deep breath, deep breath.

"Do you remember when you got Blue?"

Lila looks up at Cass and nods. Tears fill her eyes. Cass wants to take it back.

"The day the angels took my little girl away."

In the afternoon breeze the neighbour's snow white shirt floats from the clothes line, arms flailing.

"I'm sorry you lost the baby, Lila."

Lila clutches the parrot. "Well I can't be good at everything. I'm a good homemaker at least. She throws her chin up, points it towards Cass's kitchen.

Cass gazes up at where a higher spirit might be waiting to offer a helping hand. There's nothing but an old water stain in the corner of the ceiling. She needs to get out of the house. Pins and needles irritate the top of her head. Her hair feels sweaty. She shoves it behind her ears. "I don't think it's that cut and dry, Lila."

"It's not the first time it's happened. It's just that this one got a lot farther along than the rest. I know one day I'll reconcile it within myself but for now I just need some time alone, me and Blue."

She rubs the impression on her finger left by her wedding rings. The shower runs and runs. Cass dashes toward the bathroom. The hot water steams the mirror. The heat soothes her skin. She reaches into the medicine cabinet and swigs on the juice. Licks her lips and returns a little calmer to Lila, who is reclining on the mocha couch. The blue parrot watches from the mantelpiece. Cass half expects it to say, Kaw. Pretty girl.

Kaw. Kaw. Pretty girl. Then whistle. She wills it to. For a moment, she doesn't blame her sister-in-law for seeking solace in the parrot. If Lila can satisfy her maternal instinct by nurturing a blue glass parrot with a special glint in its eye created by the careful hand of a talented artisan, then so be it. Whatever it takes, whatever it takes to fill the emptiness in the womb, the echo, the hollowness, the constant nagging and nagging. No matter how much Lila may think women have changed, they can't change what their bodies are programmed for. No matter how hard they try to defy that, the body won't let a woman forget—the void grows and it grows.

"Where are your rings, Lila?"

"I sold them on the way here."

"I think we need a drink."

"I don't drink."

"That could be the root of your problems."

"You're the one with the problem."

"You don't know the half of it."

Cass strolls into the kitchen, grabs two tumblers and the bottle of Meritage that Mitch bought to boost her iron and enrich her red blood cells. Along with that and the Guinness Mitch picked up she should be back on her feet in no time. Perhaps the Cointreau is messing with her progress. She sits next to Lila and pours them each a glass of wine.

Lila looks at the grandfather clock looming in the corner.

"What is time, Lila? In lieu of everything, I mean really."

Lila scoffs.

"Do you like poetry, Lila?"

"Poetry?" She exchanges glances with the parrot. "Poetry doesn't make sense to me."

Cass sips her wine. It's the only thing that makes sense to her. "Well, perhaps this will. The French poet Charles Baude-laire wrote something like, *It is the hour to be drunken! To escape being the martyred slaves of time, be ceaselessly drunk. On wine, on poetry, or on virtue, as you wish.*"

Lila whispers to the parrot, takes a sip of wine and proceeds to tell Cass how she woke up one morning convinced that her husband would leave her for a woman with children so he wouldn't have to deal with the pain of losing them anymore, so she decided to leave him first. Cass downs her glass of wine, lets her talk. She swears that the damn parrot moves, glances over at her. Must be the light, the way the sun catches the glass.

"So I stopped at a pawn shop on the way out of town to sell my rings. I'm not sure where I'll go after I leave here. Blue and I will make a home for ourselves somewhere out there in a quiet little town."

"Lila, you can try again. You're just in shock. It's a terrible experience."

"It's too much work to try again, too painful when it falls through."

"I know. We spend half our lives trying not to get pregnant. Then when we're ready it's not so easy to get pregnant, and things can happen no one ever warned us about. I know Lila, I understand."

"No you don't. You couldn't possibly understand. We never have and never will have anything in common. Look at you."

Lila leaps to her feet and grabs the parrot, holds it close to her, rocks it. Cass swallows a few tears then wards off the violent images flashing before her eyes. She reminds herself of karma. Karma, the thing she turns to when all other mythological or religious figures let her down. Karma. She finishes her wine, taps her fingers on the side of the table and wonders if David realizes his wife has left him for good, if deep down he's relieved. Does Lila's mother know? Know about any of this? The sweet woman who had one good child, then happened to be impregnated with a demon seed.

It had only been a few weeks since Lila lost the baby. She's pale but appears healthy. How does she do it? Karma? Karma. All the same, Cass can't believe she didn't prepare for her visit. They say caring for someone else helps take your mind off your own problems. She needs something to take care of. Her husband's not home enough. When she's better she'll get an animal, a big one, like a horse. That way she'll be forced to leave the house for extended periods of time. Until then, it's all too much work, the slightest thing; brushing her teeth, her hair, pulling on her clothes, taking them off, dialing the phone. A house guest is monumental, not to mention the house. Taking on the house with character was like buying an old person and attempting to make them young again. That is monumental. The house is monumental, almost every room is incomplete. What at this time in her life should be her sanctuary is a perpetual state of confusion and there's nothing she can do about it. She can't pull the place together herself, all she can do is tell the men who know what to do what she wants and at this point she doesn't know what she wants. Paint colours? Light fixtures? Light fixtures have been the hardest thing to decide on. She knows she wants light—that she knows. A lot of light; light, just light. All she wants is light.

"You know, Lila, it's been a tough year for everyone, not just you."

"I have to go to the bathroom. I'm trying to hold it until we get to the restaurant but I can't wait any longer."

The blue parrot stares at Cass. "Go to hell," she says. "Don't become like her. I thought you were a good guy. You know, I really did think you were special. Even the goddamn glass blower said the second you took shape he knew you were special and I believed him."

She pours more wine into her glass. "You know Blue, when I met your uncle, your mom hated me. Yep, couldn't stand me. I didn't really know why. I was quite innocuous, easy going, a little too easy going I guess. Maybe I was too studious, book-ish. I like poetry. Dust doesn't bother me that much but you know the big things do. Do you understand? Do you? Thanks. Thanks, Blue."

Lila walks into the kitchen. Shakes the water from her hands then turns them into fists.

"What are you doing?" she asks.

Cass sits up straight, wipes the smile from her face.

"Nothing."

"Are you talking to my parrot?"

"No."

"You were."

"I was not. Stupid parrot. It's not real, Lila."

"You are so cruel."

Lila grabs the parrot and tucks it into her chest. "No. You're right. She's not a pretty girl. She is not a pretty girl," she cries as she runs onto the porch.

Cass slugs a mouthful of wine from the bottle. She gets up, peers out the window, then behind her where the parrot sat a moment before. The white shepherd stands at the back door of its master's house, tail wagging. Cass grabs the phone and calls the station. A duty officer answers and tells Cass that Mitch and his partner got a call out on Canyon Road they had to attend to. The officer pops her gum and says, "He said that if you called to tell you it could be a late one, that kind of call, you know." Cass nods, she's accustomed to those calls. The top of her skull aches. Her heart tightens like something's pulling at it from behind. It happens when she's unsure of whether she's being told the truth, like when a doctor tells her not to worry, even though she knows something's not right inside or times like this when she's told that

Mitch got a call out on Canyon Road. The bad end of town where all hell breaks loose at the most inopportune times like holidays and weekends and special occasions or when the contractors are being assholes or a relative comes to visit. She convinces herself she's just tired, overwrought, can't differentiate a big bad wolf from a grandmother. Nothing seems real and everything's too goddamn real. No filter, just the raw deal. Her husband is a good man. He's hurting too. She convinces herself the Canyon Road call is not a ruse he concocted so he wouldn't have to go for wine and groceries and sunflower seeds for the goddamn blue parrot he didn't like in the first place. Perhaps he's hiding out in his office so he doesn't have to face his sister, wouldn't that be just like a brother. The tightness intensifies, it numbs her heart. She runs into the bathroom and slugs some juice, grabs her stringy hair and pulls on it. "Enough," she screams. She grabs the garbage from the bathroom and goes to the basement.

Lila grasps the parrot to her chest, tells it to never, ever talk to Cass again. She stares at her left hand, studies the impression her wedding rings have left in her skin. She wonders if it will ever go away, the reminder of the bond she broke. When she sold the rings to the pawnbroker, he said they weren't worth as much as Lila believed they were. She told the guy she should get a refund from the jeweller, a full refund because they didn't live up to their role in the wedding vows. The pawnbroker stared at her and said, "Isn't it the love that should have lived up to the vows?" Lila thought about it and in the clutches of a complete and utter breakdown she released the rings and shoved them toward the pawnbroker. The guy began to count out the money. "You wanted the rings," he said. "Huh? Maybe that's all you wanted was the rings. You might as well keep 'em." She rubbed her ring finger. "Just give me the money!" she screeched.

Cass's voice floats up the basement stairs singing the same lines over and over: *Godspeed Mother Nature, I never really wanted to say goodbye. Godspeed Mother Nature, I never really wanted to say goodbye.* Lila listens for a moment then follows the tune down the stairs into the basement. It smells. Lila covers her nose with her sweater. On her hands and knees, Cass sorts through piles and piles of empty fruit containers, egg cartons, yogurt and sour cream containers, Styrofoam, soup cans, take-out coffee cups, empty toothpaste tubes, shampoo bottles. Three bins line the back wall: a blue one, a grey one and a small thin green one. Lila places the blue parrot on the washing machine and turns it toward the window. "Blue says you're sad."

"Huh?" says Cass. She continues sifting through the containers.

"What are you doing? What is all this shit?"

Cass spins around. The parrot gazes down at her, eyes squinted. She's ready to tell it to fuck off, then catches herself. It isn't real. It isn't real.

"What are you doing?"

"Look, I'm trying to sort out what is and isn't recycling, okay? You're right, I knew you were coming. I should have cleaned up and you're going to go back and tell your mother and everyone else you know what a horrible housekeeper I am. Useless. But this, among so many other things, just doesn't make sense. What kind of a world do we live in that has made something like garbage so fucking complicated. It's not just shit you don't want. No, you can't just dump your leftovers, empty containers, toilet rolls, tampons, bottles, newspapers and boxes into one big green plastic garbage bag and stick it on the curb once a week anymore. No. No. You have to figure out what goes where. Do you even know what constitutes garbage these days, Lila? I don't know what to do."

"When's the last time you put out the garbage, Cass?"

"Well, I can't answer that, Lila because I don't know what garbage is. That blue box over there, that's for anything that can be recycled, but did you know that not just anything can be recycled? Styrofoam can't go in there, and these fruit containers, they don't go in there. If I don't learn how to interpret each of these little signs underneath, I can't tell where they go. I don't know what to do anymore and the last time I messed up, the garbage man gave me shit in front of all my neighbours and the guys working on the house and I felt this big, Lila, this big. And I'd just come home from the hospital. Do you know how that felt? I was just trying to get the goddamn garbage out on time, trying to get back to normal. You know, business as usual. Even though I should have had my fucking feet up in bed looking after myself and I was humiliated because I put chicken bones in the wrong bin—so the garbage man dumped all the rotting food, chicken bones, spaghetti, coffee grinds, stinking broccoli, the soup my mother made that I just couldn't eat and dumped it all over my driveway. Then threw the green bin on my lawn and told me to read the brochure that came with the goddamn thing. Can you believe it? Humiliated by a goddamn garbage man? A goddamn garbage man that thinks he rules the world."

"You were in the hospital?"

"Look Lila, why don't you and the parrot go for a walk and I'll get this place cleaned up. Okay? Because you need somewhere to lie down and rest and eat and I'll look after you for a while? Okay? It's what we both need. All right?"

She hurls an egg carton at the wall.

"So, you haven't put out any garbage since?"

Lila glances at the parrot and raises her eyebrows. Cass follows her gaze. She swore it faced her, now it stares at the wall she hit with the egg carton.

"What would that French poet have to say about this?" asks Lila.

"He'd say, *The devil's best trick is to persuade you that he doesn't exist.*"

Lila cradles the parrot in her arms and heads upstairs. She grabs her purse and walks outside. The lilac moon hangs around with the midday sun. She lights a cigarette. The screen door squeaks. Cass joins Lila on the porch.

Mothers gather around the school to pick up their children for lunch, smiling mothers with smaller babies in strollers, some with another one growing in their bellies, happily waiting for the children to come streaming out of the school and into their open arms. Grandmothers glance over from neighbouring porches and gardens, remembering.

Lila rubs the imprint of her wedding rings. She knows David will never forgive her. Cass sips a newly filled glass of wine, looks away from the school. The parrot appears to be breathing in the warm air, content as the white shepherd asleep on the cool grass. The school bell rings. Cass counts to ten and the side doors of the building fly open. Squeals and laughter fill the air. Lila looks at Cass.

"Don't you ever wonder what it's like to be a mother, Cass?"

Cass chokes on her wine. It burns her throat.

"More than you can ever imagine. And the older I get the more I'm haunted by what's missing. Jesus, Lila. Don't you ever wonder why Mitch and I aren't parents?"

"I just figured you're selfish. You know, career people. You're a career woman."

"Career women have babies, Lila."

"Yeah, but you're a school librarian. You're around kids all day. I just figured by the time you got home you'd had enough."

"Yeah and your brother's a cop. He puts himself on the line every friggin' day for other people. How can you possibly think we're selfish?"

"Because he got married and left us. He moved away. We never see him and you're selfish because you took him from us."

"Who's us? You and your parrot?"

The kids swarm around their mothers. Boys shove each other, little girls scream. The teacher on yard duty blows a whistle and encourages the mothers to take charge of their children and move along. Lila puts out her cigarette.

"I don't know why anyone would want to be a teacher. It looks like a hell of a job."

"Maybe some people genuinely want to help kids with the arduous task of growing up."

"Isn't that what mothers do?"

"Not every woman gets to be one."

She dumps her wine in the flower bed. Lila gasps. "That'll kill them."

"I beg to differ. Come with me. I think it's time I showed you the rest of the house."

The sun reflects off the plastic wrap protecting the dining room table. They walk toward the stairs. Lila stops and grabs the roses the neighbour gave her.

"What's a laudanum habit?" asks Lila.

"An addiction to poppies."

"Oh, I wonder why she gave me roses."

They walk up the stairs. Lila looks around.

"Why did you stop fixing up the house, Cass? Money? Did

you and Mitch run out of money? I can lend you money. How the hell can you live in this mess?"

Cass grasps the banister. This mess? She can't deny that the place is a mess. It is a mess. Everything had come to a stand-still. The house is a mess because she is a mess, in need of renovation, a fresh coat of paint, lighting, support beams—there'd been structural damage. It's not so easy to rectify structural damage. Lila clutches Blue, strokes its head. Cass glances over at the parrot and nods just to piss Lila off. Lila frowns and shoves the parrot's head under her armpit.

When they reach the second floor, Cass points to where a row of pot lights will adorn the hallway, to a sketch on the wall where a new window will go. She explains that two of the bedrooms will be opened up to create one grand master bedroom with an ensuite bathroom. For now they were sleeping downstairs in the soon-to-be dining room.

They stop outside a closed door. Lila looks at her sister-in-law. "Is this the guest room?"

"Go in." says Cass. "Go on, you first."

Lila hesitates then opens the crisply painted white door with a blue moon stenciled in the centre. Light fills the pale green room. Crystals create dancing pyramids on the walls. Indigo pillows adorn a white wood cradle. Giraffes and lions and monkeys are painted along the borders and stuffed animals line the edges of the room. It's too still.

Lila clutches the parrot. She turns around to face Cass.

"You're having a baby?"

Cass shakes her head and pats her flat stomach. "Not anymore, Lila. And you thought we had nothing in common."

Tears trickle down Lila's cheeks. "I had no idea."

No one did. It ended before they were ready to spill the beans. The nursery was the first room they finished in the house when Cass had discovered they were pregnant. It was completed in a few weeks and then everything had to stop, no paint fumes, dust, lifting, and in the eleventh week the pain and the ambulance and the eight hours on a hospital gurney waiting for the gynecologist-on-call to get back from her son's baseball tournament. Cass remembers watching the other doctors and nurses pacing back and forth outside her room, glancing in at her, biting their nails, making phone calls and popping in to see if she was comfortable. She wasn't comfortable. She was in so much pain she was on the verge of panic. The nurses were on the verge of panic too, and they couldn't give her painkillers because of the baby, whatever could possibly have been left of the baby and when the gynecologist sauntered in with the nurse's ultrasound results, she informed Cass that she needed a blood transfusion because she was hemorrhaging and too much blood had collected in her bowels. They were drowning in her blood, Cass and the baby. It had been in the wrong place she told her, ectopic, Greek for the wrong place, and everything had ruptured that wasn't supposed to because the doctor watched the baseball game until the end of the seventh fucking inning.

Imagine, Cass screamed, imagine if your son had never had the chance to be born because the doctor-on-call was at a fucking baseball game. The gynecologist didn't answer, just injected Cass with morphine.

"You're right Lila, not all women are born to be home-makers or mothers. I guess I'm one of those changed women."

"Cass, I didn't mean . . . You're not that old. You can try again."

"No, Lila. I lost everything that day. I'm walking around with somebody else's blood in my veins. But you know what, I've got a great husband despite everything you did to try to mess that up and you can hang onto your little fantasy about angels and all that, but I gave you that blue parrot for your ninth wedding anniversary. And everybody knows that you got rid of your baby when you thought David was cheating on you months before you were ever scheduled to give birth, then feigned a miscarriage when the abortion went wrong just so people wouldn't learn how vile you really are. So no, actually, you are right, we have nothing in common. And while you were in the bathroom earlier, Blue told me that you never intended on staying here, that you just wanted to drop by and cause some friction between your brother and I because your perfect world got fucked up the ass, so you came here to try and fuck up mine like you've always tried to do. Well you're too late, Lila."

"Blue told you that?"

"Yes. We had a really good talk. He told me everything.

Everything you ever told him about how you've felt about me from the start. I'll tell you something Lila, you should be very careful who you divulge your secrets to. That parrot's got a mind of its own."

Lila backs out of the nursery and runs down the stairs. Cass follows her. Lila rushes around the living room looking for her bags, her purse. "Maybe you should just leave Blue with me, Lila. I may not give it a clean home, but I'll certainly give it a better life than you ever could."

Lila spins around and hurls the parrot across the room toward Cass. "No!" Cass jumps up to grab it. The parrot smashes into the fireplace. Blue glass shatters across the room. "No," whispers Cass. She swears she heard the parrot shriek.

# Colt 45

MY LONG BLONDE hair sticks out from beneath the helmet and rests on my shoulder pads. I wear jersey number 45, white boots with long cleats. The guys are congenial. Especially Manning. They bend to my level to give me pep talks, or explain why the coaches can't use me in a particular game. I appreciate their kindness. Coach Dungy assures me that he and Manning believe in my abilities. They say I'm agile, fast and sly. If it weren't for the lack of experience and possibly my weight, Coach says he'd try to put me out there more often. I'll wait. I have to pay my dues, earn the respect of the guys—and I will. I toss back and forth. In the first play of the game, Harrison is injured. Next thing I know the offensive coach slaps my ass, tells me I'm in on the next play. I twitch. Run onto the field, the crowd goes wild. My pads are heavy. I wobble with every stride. Manning rarely calls plays in a huddle formation but I think on account of starting me, he's bending his rules. His big face is in my little face and all the guys heads are an inch from my head. Their large eyes peer at me from behind their facemasks. Their heavy breathing hits my face. My heart hammers against my chest pads. I take my place at the far left of the line of scrimmage. Manning calls Milwaukie, Coca-Cola, Coca-Cola, Lego. Lego. Hup. Hup. The ball snaps from between the center's legs. I run forward then turn around at the spot I believe the ball will come flying into my ungloved hands, but Manning's being pressured by Lewis. I'm wide open. I jump up and down. "Over here," I scream. Manning remains focused. Doesn't look my way. "Come on," I scream. My arms flail. Then I look up and notice the ball flying toward me. I jump for it, fly off my feet into the calm air. I wake up in a sweat. Al holds me down, both hands pin my shoulders to the bed. His red face glares at me. I remove my mouth guard.

"What's up, honey?"

"You gotta stop this, Paige."

"They played me, hon. I was wide open."

"You're ruining my life. You've got to stop playing football in your sleep. It's killing me."

I slam my head against the pillow. Tears wet my face. I finally get my chance to prove to Manning, to the rest of the Indianapolis Colts that I am a worthy receiver and Al wakes me up, wakes me from the happiest moment of my life. He rubs his head and says, "I'm sorry, I . . ." I can't look at him. I can't. I grab my pillow, an extra blanket from the closet, run downstairs, curl up on the couch and attempt to return to the twenty yard line.

The front door slams, wakes me up. My body aches every-where, everywhere, from my fingertips to my coccyx to my big toe and everything, everything in between. Then it dawns on me. I press my fists into my thighs. I know that pain—Coach must have kept me in the game last night and I slept through it. Al interrupts one of the best dreams ever and he has the nerve to storm out of here without saying goodbye. I hate Tuesdays.

I shower, check my body for bruises, no bruises. It hurts pulling on my sweats, my T-shirt. My first client arrives at ten a.m. and I can't move, can't reach my arms to the sky or extend my toes. I grab the sweaty sheets from the bed, throw them into the laundry. I might have to get my own place. The phone rings. The cat runs under the couch. It must be Al. The next door neighbour's Baltimore Ravens flag hangs lifeless from its pole. We don't speak. I answer the phone on the last ring.

"Hello."

Al's shaky voice annoys me. He could never be a football player. I had a dream once where all the Colts came to our house for a barbecue. Most of them arrived in their uniforms, some without tops but they all had their bottoms on, towels thrown around their thick necks. Manning arrived in a suit. We drank beer, hung out in the hot tub, swam. They were funny, polite, sweet. A few of the D-line sat down with me and explained how happy they were that I was on the team. Their sincerity overwhelmed me. What a dream, and in the dream Al spent most of his time in the house peering out from behind the curtains. Embarrassment's an understatement. I don't think I moved too much in bed that night. It was a passive gathering. I never told Al about that dream.

"Paige, I'd like you to meet me after work for a drink."

The cat peers out from under the couch. We exchange glances. It's odd.

"Okay, Al," I say.

"At Busters."

"Busters? The sports bar?"

"Yeah. Say five-ish. If I'm late you can watch highlights."

I slap my forehead. The cat runs out of the room. That's so good of Al. So good of him to put my needs first after he ruins my chances of making the catch of my life that just might have put me on the NFL map. Now he wants to kiss my ass?

My client arrives with herbs and a candle. One of those lovely people that never arrive at someone's home empty handed. A gesture I find charming but unnecessary when one's paid before entering. She aims to achieve enlightenment by taking my Twelve Steps to a More Fulfilling Life program. I cautioned her that I focus on connecting with one's core—literally and metaphorically; I hope to make her happier but I can't guarantee enlightenment. We begin by sitting cross-legged on the hardwood floors facing my heavily treed backyard. I wince as I remain in this position. My energy is stilted, altered. The cat scratches against the closed studio door. My client sighs out of context.

"Are you all right?" she asks. "You seem a little preoccupied."

I'm horrified. Although I work from home, I swear I leave my personal problems at the threshold of my studio. When I'm working, I'm working. She looks into my eyes, raises her eyebrows. I like her. I cannot let my clients down. How can one come for guidance and be let down by the person who claims to be centred, the learned one who's sharing their knowledge to strengthen the student's inner being? I always meet with my clients first, conduct an interview process to establish they are serious, are not going to waste my spiritual time. In our discussion, this client told me she was a Green Bay Packers fan; a team I've always had a soft spot for. We bonded.

"No, there's nothing wrong," I say.

The cat claws the outside of the oak door. I swallow the expletives. It's part of my training, the Zen in me—control when I need it. She raises her eyebrows while keeping her spine straight, hands in Gyan Mudra. I gaze at the swaying grass. Manning never loses his cool, at times he seems flustered but that's the genius in him. If he was reactionless he wouldn't be so clever, deep. Intensity is part of his character, his passion, his wizardry; he never, ever loses his cool, not like Warner. I gaze at my fingers. They ache from the thrashing around I did in bed last night. I must have been gripping the side of the mattress, the bed posts. At times my eyes open slightly and I peer down the bed and think the bed posts are goal posts. That's where I was aiming for last night before Al woke me, straight into the end zone. Sometimes I flip back and forth into consciousness, can feel my legs flying up in the air, my body thrusting, arms flailing. I've never been aware of pummeling Al, but he swears that I knock him senseless every Sunday and Monday night. I know I don't only dream of playing for the Colts on those nights. I realize it's more intense after I've been watching football for at least twelve hours on Sunday, and Monday night is the cherry on top. It makes sense that my psyche is inundated with the shit, what the hell else could I possibly dream about? I must admit the first night I went to sleep and showed up fully dressed as an Indianapolis Colt, standing on the sideline in between Saturday and Sanders, was overwhelming. That's living the dream.

My client draws my attention to the ringing phone, tells me it hasn't stopped ringing since she arrived. I shake my head. My shoulders tense up, something someone in my position shouldn't let happen. I open my mouth. She puts her finger up to hers. "Listen," she says, "I'm at step three and you know I've learned one has to listen to the voice within, to follow one's gut, listen to yourself, be true. You have to do what you have to do, Paige."

She places her hands in prayer position and bows to me. I hold back my tears. Tell her I'll make it up to her next week. She tells me she believes this is all part of her journey, packs up her notebook and faux sheepskin mat.

I pour myself a Bud and watch the NFL network. The cat

slumbers on the couch beside me. I can't keep my eyes open. I close them and before I know it, I'm dressed in my Colt's uniform, sitting on a sideline bench next to Gonzalez, sipping Gatorade. I awake when the cat's claws jab into my sore thighs. "Christ," I say. I rush into the bedroom and grab something sexy from my wardrobe. All I've been wearing lately are my Colts sweats. I'm not sure why I feel compelled to be sexy. My boyfriend calls me up and asks me to meet for a drink after work, that's a perfectly normal thing for a man to do with the woman he's seeing, but we've been together since Dungy joined the Colts in 2001, and this is unusual. I better dress sexy.

Men and women in suits pack Busters, faces glowing, smiles bouncing off walls like everyone's been there since lunch. Why was my corporate job never like this? I order a pint of Bud. Al whisks in, kisses my cheek. The waitress flows up to our table, says to him, "Usual, Al?" He nods. I slide my *Pro Football Weekly* under my clenched ass. A man at the counter speaks loudly, something about the Seahawks. They're having a terrible season. Hasselbeck, the team, everyone misses Alexander but no one comes right out and says it. The waitress brings Al a scotch and soda. I didn't know he drank scotch and soda. His blue eyes look bruised. On the TV atop the bar, Tony Kornheiser's holding a mask of the Raven's Ray Lewis across his face, he's pointing an imaginary gun at Michael Wilbon. Al rolls his eyes.

"It's *Pardon the Interruption*, Al. You love Tony Kornheiser."

"Not so much since he joined *Monday Night Football*. I think he's stretching himself too thin."

He sips his scotch and soda. His half-closed eyes add a few years to his once wholesome face. The waitress saunters past. Al glances over at me. I hope he's taking in my tight v-neck sweater, and the makeup I put on. If the guys on the team saw me like this they'd tease me for days. Al places a book on the table, shoves it toward me. I scan the title, *Memories, Dreams, Reflections* by Jung, C.G.; Aniela Jaffe. My stomach turns. I remove my red velvet blazer.

"Al, I am more than aware of Jungian philosophy. Jesus Christ. What are you trying to do to me?"

I down my Bud, motion to the waitress to bring me another.

"Listen, Paige."

"So what are you going to say, Al? It's the Indianapolis Colts or you? Because I doubt there's a pair of Super Bowl tickets shoved into that book, Christ!"

The waitress snaps her gum and looks over at me in disdain. The bartender pours my beer while switching the channel on the TV. I gasp. He changes it back to the previous channel.

"Paige, you have a problem."

"Al, if you were smart, in this case Freud's *The Interpretation of Dreams* might have been more apt. Opposed to Jung, Freud argued that the groundwork of dreams is based on wish-fulfillment, and that the plan for the dream can almost always be found in the events of the day preceding the dream. It's very simple—don't make this more complicated than it is, Al."

"So you want to be a football player, Paige. Is that what it is? Come on. We need to get to the bottom of your dreams, Paige. I haven't slept properly all season. It's fucking with my head."

"I didn't ask for these dreams, Al. I don't make them happen." I shove the book back toward him, "Perhaps you should read up on Jung. But I know how you feel about reading, so here, let me give you an idea of what he'd say about dreams. Jung believed that the psyche is a self-regulating entity in which conscious views are likely to be offset unconsciously, in the dream, by their opposites."

Al stares into his scotch. "How do you know all that Paige?"

"Because I studied it, goddammit, who do you think I am, just some dumb jock?"

I down my beer. Al motions to the waitress to get me another.

"Paige, is it the way they look? Am I not fit enough? Am I not manly enough? Is this a latent high school dream of yours to be with some quarterback? I mean in your dreams are you really playing ball with these guys, with Manning? Huh?"

"Al!" I brace myself against the plush leather back of the booth. Al's hands tremble. His eyes pool with tears.

"Al, my God."

I stare at the TV screen. Kornheiser's interviewing Kyle Orton. Nice kid, okay quarterback. Al shakes the ice in his empty glass. I like Al, I do. This has nothing to do with Al. I can't help it. In my dreams I'm a professional football player, a wide receiver for the Colts. I'm sorry I flail around in bed, keep him up all night during the regular season. I'll have to sleep downstairs from now on. God forbid we make it to the playoffs, the Super Bowl. I'll have to get a suite at the Days Inn. Al can sleep and I'll fully realize my dreams. Then before we know it the season will be over for another six months. There's always a solution. It's part of my twelve step program. Jung would completely agree with that.

"Do you love me, Paige?"

I sip my beer.

"I want you to speak to someone about this."

"What?"

He shoves a business card toward me. If I didn't do what I do for a living, spend hours in meditation, assist troubled souls seek solace in the joys of one's being, in nature, in the complexities of life itself, I would have thrown my beer at him and stormed out of that damn cougar sports bar. But I can't. I can't. I agree to go to one session with the psychologist he looked up in the phone book. But Al has to read Freud.

The doctor's waiting room is white. All white. White couch, white chairs, white walls. No plants. So contrived. Thank God for the vibrant *Sports Illustrated* magazines on the glass table. The receptionist calls my name. I look around the empty room, get up and follow the petite woman into the doctor's office. He stands up to greet me. His hand is clammy as it shakes mine. He pulls away from my firm grip.

"Strong," he says.

He should feel how I grip a football. I sit down. He flips through a folder, must be full of Al's comments. Keeping his head down, he places his elbows on his desk, rubs his hands together in front of his face.

"So, Paige, you're a wide receiver for the Indianapolis Colts?"

Oh Christ. "Well, kind of, doc, when I'm not teaching people to embrace their inner being." If he only knew how much we have in common.

"And what are these dreams like, Paige."

Oh Christ. "Are you a football fan, doc?"

"Yes."

"You are? That's great. Who's your team?"

"The New England Patriots."

"No guff? That Cassel's stepped up to the plate, huh."

The doctor peers over his spectacles. Of course he peers over his spectacles.

I proceed to tell him how the dreams are more or less how the games happen on TV. Except there's no instant replay or crazy camera angles. I'm mostly on the sidelines, but every now and then I get to play, kind of like how the Chargers use Darren Sproles. Everything pretty much happens like in real life, except I'm a chick and I play for the Colts. The doctor stops writing in his pad and looks up at me. I shrug and continue to explain that the team doesn't treat me like a chick though; to them I'm one of the guys. "There's not too much else to tell you," I say. "At night when I tuck myself in and drift into my subconscious I play football. Simple, and apart from the fact that my boyfriend takes the brunt of my tackles and loses sleep over it, I have a really great night's sleep. I wake up really, really happy. Sore, but happy. I get to do something I'd never have the chance to do consciously."

"When did you first start having these dreams, Paige?"

"Oh, I don't know, just after Dungy came on board and Manning started making a name for himself as one of the greatest quarterbacks going—a few years now. It's Manning that I really look up to. I've followed him since college. He's a wizard you know. A real scientist. When he started his no-huddle thing, I thought I was going to die. It's completely unnerving but really, really exciting. I think it was around that time that I woke up one morning and went whoa, last night I played for the Colts."

The doctor writes in his notebook. I don't even care what he's writing. I'm not the insecure one. I look out the window at the half-lit sky. Rain spits against the window. I think about the weekend's games, about how the moment Tuesdays hit I look forward to the next Sunday and the next. During the NFL season, Sundays are sacred. I'll never forget this one Sunday when Al I first started dating. I knew Al had a beef with me over something. It brewed in the whites of his eyes, made them yellowish, hazy. His mouth began to open. I shook my head, pressed my hands together. I warned him that if he uttered one word, I would fall on my knees and pray that he shuts up. I would go that far. Then I'd scream like a banshee until he shut up. Sundays from September until February are sacred. I refuse to let anything bring me down.

"It's not just in my dreams, doc. It's everything. I love football. My weekend football routine makes life worth living. I drink my coffee while perusing the stats. I'm part of a friend's office football pool, which I've won three years in a row and I play Proline, a habit much like smoking or drinking. Not overly healthy and highly addictive, I know. I re-evaluate my picks, take a quick glance at the *USA Today's* NFL section, study analysis of every game, pick up on any important information that I may have missed, a probable, an injury, a rivalry. I study NFL.com, watch all the pregame shows to make sure there are no last minute changes. I check the weather from Boston to San Diego, which way the wind's blowing at certain stadiums like Lambeau Field, Soldier Field, Texas Stadium, Giants Stadium, Candlestick Park, Heinz Field, Arrowhead, Ralph Wilson and home turf, Lucas Oil Stadium. Weather is very important. Especially if a team like the Miami Dolphins is on the road against the Buffalo Bills in January, wind coming off the water, snow squalls, minus ten degrees. It's not a given but every factor counts in a game like that when you're betting. Doc, football makes me happy."

I gaze at the doctor. He gazes back. He's a Patriots fan. He's probably not listening to a word I'm saying. I think of Al, his selfishness. It's early in the season and teams are just starting to break from the pack. The pressure, intensity, the drama, it's only going to get more complex. If Al wants me to make a decision, I'm going to have to risk it. The doctor leans forward in his chair. He opens his mouth to say something but I stop him.

"You know, my relationship has become like a game, doc. It's the two minute warning, I'm down by a field goal, fourth and ten. What would Manning do? He'd go for the touchdown, doc, and then goddammit he'd go for the two point conversion. I'm not going to give up on being an Indianapolis Colt. There's no way. We've got one life, doc. I have to follow my dreams. I can't control my subconscious, but I can control my love life."

"You know, Paige, Al's damn lucky to be with a woman like you. Someone so passionate about football. You're a find, Paige. I wish my wife were more like you. She can't stand the game."

"Yeah, well, she probably doesn't keep you up at night."

A little bell goes off and the doctor tips his glasses to the end of his purple nose and says he'll see me the same time next week. I'm horrified. I can't imagine what we'll talk about. I place my hand on the door knob. The doctor clears his throat, calls my name. I wait a second then turn around. He looks down for a moment. Then gets up and walks toward me, rubs a finger across his thick grey moustache, clears his throat again. I nod, wait for him to quote some Jungian passage that will tug on my guilt strings. I feel lonely, like it's beginning to rain inside.

"I was just wondering. Who are you taking in this weekend's Pittsburgh-San Diego game?"

I laugh. My heart warms, tears well up in my eyes.

"What's the spread?" I ask.

"I think Pittsburgh's favoured by nine."

"By nine, huh? Well, I don't know, doc. Rivers is a crafty bugger, but Roethlisberger's a bulldozer. Keep an eye on the weather."

I walk out the door. Wink at the receptionist. Tell her I'll see them the same time next week.

## About the Author

**Alexandra Leggat** is the author of two previous collections of short fiction, *Pull Gently, Tear Here* (nominated for the Danuta Gleed First Fiction Award), *Meet Me in the Parking Lot*, and a volume of poetry entitled *This is me since yesterday*. As well as being a freelance writer and editor, she teaches creative writing classes through the University of Toronto School of Continuing Studies and lives in Toronto.